THE
DEADLIEST EQUATION

Race kept remembering how Jacaranda had lit up in an instant from the flash of his shot. He had the kind of powers that laid planets waste.

Sitting there, scowling at the dead world, he let his mind drift back to his peasant days when the mere thought of Starlings had caused him to tense. He knew now that in every human sense they were no different from the peasants.

That was the terrifying thing.

Those stern, shining faces of his fancy were just the product of youthful ignorance. This planet had been destroyed by uncontrolled emotions, by Starling emotions.

I've got to watch myself, he thought, *my own home world could wind up like this.*

Power plus whimsy is the deadliest equation.

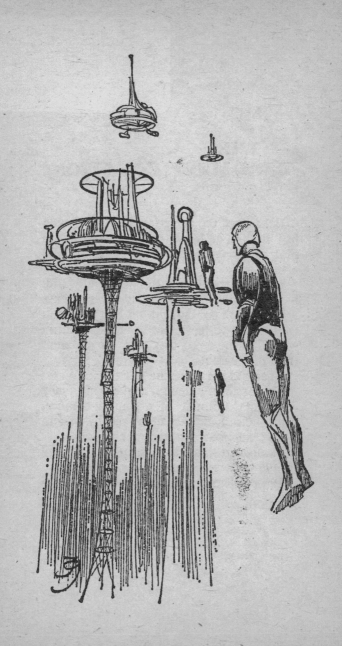

The Star-Crowned Kings

Robert Chilson

DAW BOOKS, INC.

DONALD A. WOLLHEIM, PUBLISHER

1633 Broadway, New York, NY 10019

PUBLISHED BY
THE NEW AMERICAN LIBRARY
OF CANADA LIMITED

First Printing, August 1975

4 5 6 7 8 9

DAW TRADEMARK REGISTERED
U.S. PAT. OFF. MARCA
REGISTRADA. HECHO EN U.S.A.

PRINTED IN CANADA
COVER PRINTED IN U.S.A.

1

Race gasped! The flagstone before the cottage door had lifted obediently into the air some six inches—to the height it should have had above the grass. Race was vaguely conscious of a quivering tension within him. His mounting fear broke in that gasp and the tension broke with it: the flagstone fell back with a faint sound. Race lifted a white face to his mother's.

"What happened?" she asked sharply.

"Th-the flagstone . . . raised up. . . ." His voice was a croak.

Janinda Worden stepped to the open half-door and looked down at it, a tiny frown between her brows. She was still slim and youthful and attractive, her face as now usually serious. There was fresh black earth about the edges of the flagstone and the grass blades had been bent outwards on all sides.

"Come inside." Janinda glanced left, then right, at the empty street of Ravenham. The village was as quiet as usual.

"Tell me about it."

Race was still in shock; he seated himself lest his legs give way. "Well, you know, we've always wanted that flag lifted, and I just looked at it and wished it was higher, like I've done a-a hundred times, and—and—"

The stone was too low, and ever since he had stepped into a puddle almost ankle deep over it, it had irritated him. But it was so big that it would take the three of them to lift it—or more. So they had never gotten around to raising it. It hardly seemed to matter; life was placid in Ravenham.

Janinda was different from the rest of the villagers. She had gone through youth, marriage, childbirth, and widowhood without much change in her matter-of-fact demeanor, but there was something more than mere placidity within her. That was comforting just now. To Race's relief his mother accepted his statement as calmly as she accepted everything.

"Could you do it again?"

Icy fingers plunged into his belly. "I-I don't—know." Race felt that he had turned white.

Janinda did not press him. After a thoughtful moment she said, "All right, we won't discuss it any more, for the moment. Don't tell Joss about it—or anyone else, naturally. It's not at all impossible, you know," she said gently.

Race gulped, nodded, if anything more frightened than before. All his short life he had known of Starlings. They could, and routinely did, move mountains by their thoughts alone. Working together, they could and had moved planets. They alone could propel starships across the galaxy and hence deserved the name *Starling*—children, dwellers, of the stars.

They were the god-like figures who dwelt in the spires they raised, who crossed the sky occasionally in the gleaming cars they moved with their minds, distant bright points of awe, who ruled Mavia and Sonissa and the Imperial Cluster, and all the stars back to legendary Earth from which they all sprang, human and Starling. Their rule was iron, their will law, their whim death or wealth to the mere humans who orbited about them.

Race retired to his room in a daze. Two emotions warred in him. One was fear. He imagined himself the butt of his schoolmates—how they would laugh that anyone from Ravenham, especially a Worden, could be a Starling!—and of course it couldn't be true. No, better never mentioned. Then in a breath he imagined himself confronting a scornful-eyed, imperious Starling with a crown on his head, trying to gain admittance to *their* society. From the expression on the Starling's face, never. . . .. His comfortable life was torn apart and nowhere could he turn.

The other emotion was elation. While his fears rose and fell so did exultation. He saw himself flying above his worshipful schoolmates, saw himself raising his own Spire, dressing his mother and sister in gold-shot glass, building his own ship and plunging into the galaxy beyond the Cluster. . . .

Jocela Worden laughed at her brother when Race dragged himself to the table. The shadows were long outside, the air slightly cooler, with a hint of the evening's dew. It had been the longest afternoon of his life.

"You shouldn't have been in such a hurry to grow up," Joss said mischievously. "If you think you're tired now, wait till harvest!"

Race had recently gone to work under Keithly in the great grassfields served by Ravenham: the village was a proprietary one, one of many on the S. (Starling) Oroné plantation. The fields were the destiny of most of Ravenham youth, those who could not escape to Fulvia or some other town. But though the work on the big tractors was tiring, it was not enough to make him sleep all day.

Joss attacked a meager portion of fruit salad and slanted her impish eyes at him. "Or was it an interview with Else Hann that sent you to bed? I could've told you a week ago she was going to Paulfields with Joe Gippert. . . ."

Jocela was almost two years younger than he. Race got no help from his mother. But she was not smiling faintly at their banter, as she usually did.

"How *do* you like your job with Keithly?" she asked.

He had been driving a tractor for two weeks now and she had had sense enough not to ask that. Race looked at her, wondering what could be behind the question. "All right, I guess. It sure cuts into my time."

Five and one-half days a week, ten hours a full day,

he drove a monstrous steam tractor pulling a six-bottom gangplow across the bright green fields, turning the tall grass into—not under—the rich soil, to make it yet richer for the next crop of grass. All summer he expected to be driving the same tractor, now cutting the grass to be baled or pickled as ensilage. The protein-rich green gold was the starting point for a whole series of syntheses, some of them taking place in animal bodies, some in great vats full of bacteria or algae. Milk, meat, wool, horn and a half a dozen other organic products came from it directly; converting it would produce food for a thousand strains of bacteria and algae that further produced hundreds of raw materials or finished products—ultimately it would end up as paper, plastics, clothing, even food.

The great fields literally extended over the rim of the planet; Ravenham set in its little private forest was an island lost in a green sea broken only here and there by the rocks of tractor and implement sheds. To a man working across them on even the tallest machine, they seemed endless. They literally *were* endless. Race would doubtless spend his life plowing and mowing them, hours looking toward the green/green horizon over an orange-painted hood, to die and be burned and scattered over them in the end.

For all its beauty, for all its placidity, Ravenham was a place of desolation and desperation.

"How does Keithly treat you?"

"Well enough, I guess."

Sometimes when the black-bearded foreman looked at him, Race thought he was mad—driven insane by the endless green plain, by the endless barren vista of life. A gruff, sullen, short-spoken sort, who seemed to like him not at all; but Keithly liked no one so far as Race could tell.

"He has you up on a tractor?"

Race nodded. Few instructions were needed, he had learned all he needed to know the first day, except how to tell his way about the fields. He had felt honored and been proud to say that he was driving. He greatly preferred it to the sheds and shops where he was directly under Keithly's eye and among the other older men, though he might pick up a trade there. But he knew what she meant. Officially he was still an Apprentice—at one-third the pay of a full Operator—though doing the latter's work.

"Plowing is easy—but cutting and baling and all take more skill. Likely he'll put the men on that and pull me back to the sheds. To learn a trade."

"Not likely," said Joss coolly. "He'll keep you on as Operator all your life—at Apprentice's pay as long as he can."

Race shifted, half-angry. "Why should he do that?" he said, trying to argue himself out of the same opinion. "It's no money in *his* pocket." Payment was by computer; Keithly couldn't quietly promote him to full Operator without telling him to pocket the difference.

"May not be Keith's doing at all—maybe the Plantation has all the Techs it needs. But Keithly will keep you an Apprentice the full year just on general principles." Joss could be unpleasantly intelligent at times.

Janinda said, "Some men are that way—even some women. They resent younger people just because they *are* younger. They don't like to realize that some day they'll be dead, and youngsters they've bawled out as dirty-faced boys will be as important as they ever were."

That remark illuminated Keithly's character like a lightning flash. Race put down his spoon slowly, feeling the horizons closing in around him. He had considered Ravenham lightly when thinking of his future. Without much thought he had long ago decided that he would be one of the lucky few who escaped to Fulvia, or even to one of the cities; in his favorite daydreams he got a job on a spaceship—a starship—even became a favorite of a Starling.

In his earlier daydreams the Starling had been a wise older man not unlike the father Race could barely remember. Nowadays she was usually a beautiful young girl, spoiled but admiring his homely wisdom.

Now, for the first time it hit home that he would probably spend the rest of his life in this house and the fields around. For excitement, the usual holidays and maybe a trip to Fulvia once a year. The tractor Race drove: it was far older than he, yet he could spend the rest of a long life driving it, and his grandson could make a good start in life on it. The big steamers rarely wore out. Ravenham was a trap that had caught him, despite all his dreams.

"It's no place to bring up children—the Plantation," said Janinda unexpectedly. "I tried to get your father to leave, long ago."

Joss was amazed. "With a wife? You'd have starved! What chance would he have of being hired by the Transport Company?"

"No worse than anyone's—hardly any, that is. It would have been hard on both of us. I've always blamed myself for ruining his life."

They could only stare at her. Janinda had never talked this way before. She looked a little past them, her face seeming soft even in the harsh glare of the fluorescent light.

"He would have left Ravenham, like his uncle did, if he hadn't fallen in love with me. But he was afraid that if he left, he'd never make it back—he knew I'd wait for him as long as necessary, it wasn't *that* he was afraid of. But you go where the Company sends you, and the best-paying jobs are mobile. And Jayce was an impatient young man, more so than most—wanting to leave was a fire in him. He couldn't wait to be married, either. I gave in—I was young too—but I was afraid it was a mistake all along."

She sighed. "Then we were married and he didn't dare take the chance—even the lucky ones sometimes have to wait months for an opening. Then you were on the way Race, and your father began to lose hope. We thought—he thought—that the Transport Company wasn't the only way out of Ravenham. There are the Plantation factories, for instance. But they are so far away—and we both had gotten old enough to lose faith in miracles. We probably wouldn't have had a chance. I told him I'd follow wherever he went and never blame him however bad things were, but he saw too clearly that it was hopeless.

"Can anyone blame him for drinking too much at times? I never did. He wasn't a regular drunk, it was only every couple of weeks, and he never so much as raised his voice to me. It never interfered with his work. He hadn't been drinking the night before he fell off his tractor. He wasn't hungover that morning, and he never drank on the job." She paused for a long time.

"He would never have gone off and left me—intentionally. Yet, I imagine he must have greeted the plowshares with relief." There was a long silence. Race and Jocela looked at each other soberly.

"When he died I swore I would escape with you both, if it meant all three of us jumping into the canal." Janinda looked into their astonished faces. "I think it's now time to leave."

Race's heart leaped, stirred by the story. In the closed society of Ravenham the facts had long been known to him. But he had never heard his mother's account of it and had not had the wit to see her viewpoint of the facts. Jayce Worden had been a wild young man who ended as could be expected: what else, in anyone so mad as to want to leave Ravenham? Race had resented that, but not consciously enough to re-examine the story. Now he was thrilled by the idea of escape as a fitting last act to that (he now saw) romance. Then the uncertainties took over.

For the well-behaved (were there any others?), life in Ravenham was as secure as could well be imagined. At no time was food short. Though there was little money, still less was the opportunity to spend it. Steady work and congenial homes were theirs by right of birth.

The Oroné were mild masters. The proprietary villagers were not well-paid, but neither were they overtaxed; a small charge for the houses was all. Involuntary projects were unknown on the Plantation. In three generations no Starling had been to Ravenham, and that had been for a ten-minute visit. There was no fear of the whims of their masters. No human overlords squatted in their Great Chairs of Justice in the square. No leather-clad patrols roamed the streets. No extortion squads harried the fortunate into dungeons. No assassins marked off the potential troublemakers.

The Plantation villages were beautifully designed. Huge old trees shaded the old houses, the latter seeming as solid, and solidly rooted, as the former. Stone and brick, with heavy slate or stone-slab roofs, built to last forever and having made a good start on it—Ravenham was picturesque with well-built age and moss and flowering vines over the brick and stone, the great trees over all. On the south, from whence came the shearing winds of winter, was a solid belt of cedars. The village faced north, toward the distant blue line of the Mountains of the Oroné.

Comfortable houses, garden fields, community barns, a meeting house, local self-government which the foremen and Plantation overseers were not permitted to dominate: they were as well cared for as prize cattle.

To leave Ravenham would mean going to Fulvia—a quiet canal-port, living mostly on the export of grass and grass products, but a fast, dangerous city to the villagers. Here, with what money they had accumulated, they would live until, somehow, a job was found. And in Fulvia the only source of jobs was the Transport Company—there was not even a row of dives. Towns like Fulvia were common in Plantation country; not every tenth one was big enough to interest the mariners of the canals.

"A woman alone would have no chance." said Janinda quietly. "It would mean a job in a private home—and even in Fulvia, that could mean anything.

Saved-up money would not last long—prices are high there, and wages low here. I have some. Very little."

That was understandable. Joss stirred resentfully. "They should have done better by you! I would by my daughter, even if I couldn't stand her."

Janinda's decision to marry one of the wild Wordens had dismayed her stolid family. Jayce was the worst of all. Didn't everyone know how wildly he talked of leaving? And didn't everyone know what happened to people who left? Why, not one in ten was ever heard of again! And them as came back were never good for anything again.

The result was the virtual disinheritance of Janinda. Her family could have gotten her a good job with the Plantation in Administration or Accounting—the Sturtevants were an old, large, respectable family in the village. The best she had been able to get was a minor job in Accounting—tallyman. That because of the tradition that all be cared for. Of advancement there was no chance.

As a widow with children, the Oroné permitted her the house for but two-thirds the usual charge, deducted from her pay by the computers in Plantcontrol. But in the early years, when the little family had had no one to hoe in the communal fields, she had to buy all their food. She could not have been saving money for as long as ten years.

"It was almost worth being dropped, not to be preached at," said Janinda cooly. Race grinned a little; his friends were always being lectured by parents, grandparents, great-grandparents, uncles, aunts, great-uncles, great-aunts—and friends of all these. He was a wild Worden boy and came in for comparatively little lecturing, but much head-shaking.

"But how long can we live in Fulvia on it? Or—" Joss caught her breath—"can we take passage to Junction City?"

"I doubt it, three of us? No. I've had years to think, though. I think we should go north."

They caught their breath. The S. Oroné Plantation was a broad valley, over sixty miles wide, oriented from northwest to southeast. At the south was a range of old hills, the stubble of a mountain range; to the north, a range of mountains parallel to it. The valley, once quite hilly and varied, had been leveled by the Oroné into a rolling, nearly flat floor a hundred and fifty years ago. The river that had flowed through it had been straightened and its drop lessened, to give it the gentlest of flows, so that the barges should not have to battle a strong current. The valley's length was about four times its width and the river, or main canal, was about forty miles from the Mountains of the Oroné to the north, twenty from the hills to the south.

Since Ravenham was but ten or twelve miles from the river—near enough to make trips to Fulvia possible —they were some thirty miles from the mountains.

"How could we live in the mountains?" Jocela's voice was hoarse.

"We have your grandfather's rifle and a good supply of shells. And Race is a pretty good shot." Wild animals grazed the grasslands and the Plantation encouraged their hunting. "We can raise a small garden—I've been accumulating seeds. We'll make out. How long it will take to cross them we can't know. And no one knows what's on the other side."

Mavia did not waste communication channels on the entertainment or education of mere humans. On the Plantation they had no certain means of learning of distant lands.

Janinda stood up briskly. "I hadn't intended to leave for, oh, nearly a month. It'll still be chilly in the mountains. But now, I think we'd better leave tomorrow." She looked at Race.

2

Race lay awake long that night. He felt as the sod must feel when the plow comes and stands it on end, one edge to the sky, the green tops on one side and the cut roots on the other. All in one day, came a shake-up such as few of Ravenham's placid people experienced in all their lives. And it came as he was still adjusting himself to the life of an equipment Operator on the great green fields.

In the cozy feelings of the dinner table and the later talk, he had forgotten about the movement of the flagstone. His mother's words brought it all back again, and now that he had time to rest after the excitement of packing he almost trembled at the possibilities.

As was her habit, Janinda had come to bid him goodnight. "Race? We'll not tell Joss about you until we're in the mountains. Not that I think she can't keep a secret—but she'll have enough to think about. And we don't know if it means anything."

"All right. I'd just as soon not talk about it—it sounds so . . . weird."

"I don't think she'd laugh, even if you can't do it again. That's another reason for going to the mountains."

"To have room to practice—yes. I hadn't thought of that."

Practice! Why, Janinda must really believe he could do it! Long he lay awake, now believing, now despairing; now hoping it was true, now fearing that it was.

15

The next morning was Sunday. The Wordens were up by first faint light, an hour before the sun. Already the village was beginning to stir. Church service was held on Sunday, for the less than half who attended on any given Sunday. Religion was not an important part of such monotonous lives as these; men who worked six days a week saw nothing wrong in taking a frequent Sunday to hunt, fish, or go on a short trip. They would have company on the road.

Race carried the rifle and quite a supply of shells. All three had packs of food and blankets wrapped in tarpaulins—discarded implement covers, common in the villages. A few cooking utensils completed their outfit, and clothes. Race felt obscurely ashamed to be carrying so much more than the usual pleasure-seekers, and Janinda appeared to share this feeling; she was anxious to be off.

They were the first out of the village. It seemed much lighter, out from under the great trees; then it seemed immensely daunting. The road seemed both endless and deadly monotonous. Overhead, the Imperial Cluster had long since set, but other stars were still visible. They faded as Ravenham shrank behind them.

The road was hard-packed earth; the usual traffic was steam tractors pulling trailerloads of hay and silage out, and manure coming in. Rides could be hitched on weekdays, but there was no specific passenger traffic; no tractor traffic at all on Sunday.

The sky turned from gray-black to deep blue to deep green. Then the sun began to rise behind them, and as the world brightened the sky began to assume its normal apple-green, a deeper color near the zenith. It looked yellow around the sun, and when Race looked back at Ravenham, southeast of them, he saw it as a dark green blot against the dazzle of yellow, set in the rich light green of the fields.

None felt like speaking. They marched in a grass-green circle bisected by the brown road, under a sky-green dome. No other road was visible from this angle—the grass was shoulder high. Little by little, Ravenham dropped below the curve of the planet. The only break in the monotony was the colorful specks of travelers far behind them in the road.

At length—some three hours of steady walking—Paulfields loomed up before them. This was a larger village but otherwise quite like Ravenham, fronting on a transverse canal and serving as a shipping point for half a dozen villages. To it they shipped the grass they raised; from it they got back manure and such food, tools, and manufactured items they could not produce themselves, plus tractor fuel. The Wordens were reasonably familiar with Paulfields, had friends and even relatives here.

Now they avoided the canal-front center of the village, where they might meet people they knew, swinging north around the edge of the village to the canal above it.

"Wow!" said Jocela in relief, dropping her pack and throwing herself down in the shade. "I never knew blankets were so heavy."

"I'm hungry."

"It might be better to go easy on the food," said Janinda expressionlessly. "It may have to last us a long time."

That made them feel twice as hungry, but both of her children stared at her in awe. No one ever had to economize on food; the necessity of rationing it had never occurred to them.

The transverse canal made a double slash of shade across the endless fields. Both sides were lined with trees, now quite old and huge. It was a placid stream. Like the river, it was designed to minimize fall and current speed; one of many graded and regulated tributaries coming down from the mountains or up from the southern hills. Like the river, these canals were string-straight and were controlled by dams at their heads. The grassfields were so skillfully managed that they had

little runoff, and that seeped evenly into the canals—
there were no streams winding through the fields.

On the water side of the trees, on each side of the
canal, was a stone-slab road typical Starling make.
Each slab was yards thick and usually more than a
hundred feet long; a mountain had been sliced into
chips to make a road. The joints between chips, however, were frequently several inches wide. The Starlings
had not patience for careful work, though in their defense it might be said that there were thousands of
miles of such roads in the Plantation.

Now the occasional fishermen pulled in their lines
and stepped back across the road; the Wordens heard
the ding-a-ling of bells. A barge train came nosing past
the town, pulled by an electric locomotive on the canal
road. The Wordens gathered up their packs without
haste; this was a familiar sight to them. The locomotive's brave scarlet and violet paint was dingy close up,
but it was massive enough to be impressive. The Operator looked languidly at them. Its speed was a little faster than a walk.

Behind came the lead barge, covered. The next barge
was silage, also covered. Then another, and another, of
the special silo barges. Finally a barge-load of hay. It
was early for hay; even the silage was only just being
brought in. But hay went upstream all the time—there
were a dozen barges of it behind this one.

Janinda led them across the grooved road—the rub-
ber tires of the engines had cut the grooves too deep in
their century and a half of operation, so the bottoms of
the grooves had been repaved with cobblestones—and
down to the edge of the canal. Joss leaped for the
barge-load, clutching the timbers of the rack with a
laugh. Race followed. His baggage hampered him more
than he had thought, and the rifle got in his way. Janinda prudently seized a rack timber and stepped down
onto the front fender wheel.

The right bank was always the near bank,
whichever way you faced, so that the barges needed

wheels on but one side to fend them off the canal side. These were about two feet in diameter, rubber-tired. Each horizontal fender wheel was covered with a wooden shield; too many people had been injured stepping onto the hub.

It would take an impossible number of guards to prevent such joyrides, so neither the Plantation authorities nor the Transport Company tried it. No one on the banks paid any attention to the Wordens.

Joss and Race clambered rapidly up the towering load, to the top of the timber rack, on up the pyramid of five-hundred-pound bales of hay. They dropped their packs with a sigh and looked eagerly around. The load was as big as a house, but was still overshadowed by the huge trees on the shore.

With a guilty start Race remembered his mother and started down to help her, but Janinda had reached the top of the rack and pulled herself easily and gracefully up despite her bundle and the umbrella. Atop the load she brushed her hair back, smiled and waved to a boy on the bank who was delighted to see a grown woman on a hayride, and looked around with pleasure.

"It's been years since I went on a joyride. I had almost forgotten what it was like."

"Don't you just love it in spring?" Joss asked eagerly.

"Yes, or in early winter when the banks are full again and it's not too cold."

"This breeze is nice, and we won't need the umbrella for hours yet."

The sensation of steady if slow movement was irresistible, so rarely did they ride a powered vehicle. Race would have been entranced even if he were not used to his tractor, though it went faster than this, twice as fast with a full gangplow. The faint hum of the distant locomotive was all but drowned by the lap of the waves between barge and bank; those were the only sounds. They knew that this motion would continue without a break to the head of the canal.

"We should be about halfway there by noon," Janinda said.

Race looked at Joss; excitement lit their eyes. Surely nobody from Ravenham had gone more than halfway there; they had to allow time for the return journey, as the barge trains on the transverse canals did not run by night.

"The farthest I ever went was two hours up," said Joss.

"Me too—to Moreton."

Both had been downstream to Fulvia on the river several times, but didn't care to mention it in their mother's presence. She knew it though, and smiled in her way, as if to herself. No one went alone, and no group could keep a secret; mothers always knew. It was not usually forbidden, but everyone knew that it was better to stay away from the town, where village gossip had so little restraining influence.

Janinda opened her bundle, rolling the tarp out on the hay first, then the blanket and the two quilts; a bedspread on top. "I wish we had more sheets," she murmured. Race wished for pillows.

Joss jabbed the folded umbrella into the hay, ready for use. It was twice as old as their mother—half as old as the Plantation, almost. Their grandmother had put a new tarpaulin cover on it about the time of their parents' marriage, so it was still in fine shape, its gold and black hardly faded.

They all sat decorously for awhile, watching the endless fields passing by beyond the trees. Then Joss and Race got restless. They prowled over the load, shouted insults at friends they saw on barges behind, and went down to drink from the clear, cool canal. They swung off and ran ahead, to climb trees and drop on the load, and for awhile they played king of the mountain on the load, though neither could swim.

They sat dumb and decorous whenever they passed a village on their side of the canal, being warned in advance by the fishermen. At each village the locomotive climbed a stone bridge over the harbor entrance, paying out cable from the boom to the lead barge. Though the engine never slowed, this allowed the barges to do so. There was time for the villagers to leap aboard and unshackle the covered barges on the end. In midstream a steam tug awaited, with a line of new barges to be attached.

Race explained the system to Joss, though she understood it as well as he. "The main idea is never to stop the locomotives; constant stopping and starting is not good for their guts. You notice that they always break the train just after the hay and silo barges. That lets each village put its own grassers on with the rest. At each village we drop a line of covered barges and pick up a different line dropped by the previous train; the train that follows us will move our covered barges up to the next village."

"Gee, thanks for telling me! I always wondered—if you knew. —It takes days for a covered barge to make it up the canal, except for the specials at the front end." The specials went straight to the canal-head villages.

"Yes, but it doesn't matter."

The covered barges carried articles for the village stores, except the tankers of tractor fuel. They were also classified as "covered" for convenience, to distinguish them from the "grassers" of hay and silage, though the latter were also covered.

Presently several men stepped off the engine and were replaced by men waiting on the road. A village lay across the stream here. The barges jolted as the tail was cut out, jolted again as the tug pushed its train against them. They saw the locomotive crew leap onto the tug's deck.

"What does that mean?"

Janinda looked at the sun. It was not yet quite overhead, but the band of shadow on the canal was quite narrow. Rays of sunlight were becoming frequent, stabbing down between limbs.

"I suppose it means we're halfway from river to mountains, and the crew is changing off to ride back down to home."

"Then these men—" Joss gestured at the engine—"they're from the mountains?"

"I suppose so."

All three looked eagerly up the string-straight canal. The Mountains of the Oroné were much taller than they had ever realized, but as ghostly blue as ever.

"We're still not halfway from home."

At her words Race and Joss sighed. The trip was becoming monotonous, and the heat was yet to come. They felt shy about jumping off the barge under the noses of these mountain men, as if they might be ordered off the hay if they disturbed anyone. But the barge behind theirs had also acquired riders, and so had several others—all strangers.

"Imagine living here in the middle of the canal, where you don't have time either to go down to Fulvia or up to the mountains on a trip," said Joss.

The merrymakers behind them began to sing, and it started them all to find that it was a perfectly familiar song.

"Going home must be more fun than coming up here—or up there, anyway," Race said, pointing to the mountains.

"Why? Oh!"

Hay went only upstream. Downstream, on the other side of the canal, came the "grassers", the flat hay barges now loaded with manure. It was seasoned, but still the commingled manures of a score and a half of domesticated animals produces an astonishing odor, one that takes getting used to. It didn't hamper romance.

For four weary hours, that afternoon, they watched the mountains climb toward the sky before them, watched the shadow band along the opposite shore widen and reach toward them. Those were the only changes for most of that time. Then, during the last hour they noticed another.

The whole valley had been given the same gentle slope as the canal, so that the bank was always the same height above the surface of the stream. Now, as they entered what had been the foothills, that careful relationship began to alter, the banks growing higher. It was visible proof that they neared their goal.

The western band of shadow never reached them. Before it could, the canal ended, abruptly, in a smooth stone face down which tumbled a sheet of water. They felt a final jolt as they were cut loose from the engine. A waiting barge swept in—the canal-head pool was three times the usual width, and it had plenty of room to maneuver—and pushed them beneath the stone bridge. This was a wider bridge than most, divided by a pier; out the other half came a train of empty barges.

There was plenty of time to watch. Across the canal to their left was another harbor entrance and another village. Trains were being made up there for the trip down in the morning; empties to be returned, other barges full of meat, hides, and the organic raw materials of the great vats. The locomotive that had brought them passed over the bridge, turned smartly to the left and passed over another bridge between them and the waterfall, to disappear among the buildings around the harbor to the left, waiting for the trip down in the morning.

It drew their attention to the waterfall. After a long stare, Janinda said softly, "It must be a dam—a rock placed to hold back water, to keep the canal the same level."

It was monstrous—a mountain—reaching halfway to the sky. They were seeing it from near its foot, and they were from the plains. It puzzled Race vaguely that he could still see the tops of the mountains over it. It was all of a hundred feet high, pierced by rows of holes. The top two were open or partly open, water cascading from them; the pressure of the water in the full reservoir closed the others. Atop the dam was another slab bridge; under it overflow water could spill down; on it were trees and houses. Very fine, large houses; the houses of Authorities.

The village harbor was gigantic—ten times as large as the ordinary village pool. A few barges were visibile at docks. There were more tugs than barges in sight; theirs was one of the first trains to reach the head of the canal. A tug cut in ahead of them, a man leaped off lithely, unshackled the covered barge ahead of them, gave them a brief wave, and shackled it to the tug. It was pushed aside to a dock.

Behind them, the train was broken up, hay and ensilage separated. The hay barges were pushed through a cavernous door into a monstrous building. The joyriders on the barges behind them waved and shouted to the crowd on the docks and steps, gathering up their things. The Wordens were all ready to disembark—they wished acutely that they had done so before the engine cast loose.

The barges' sides grated against the dock within the building and their drift slowed. Movement caught his eye and Race peered up into the gloom, to see huge steel teeth descending on them.

"All off, passengers!" called a cheery voice from the dock. "How was the trip?"

The Wordens descended, feeling clumsy and out of place. Janinda's cheeks were pink. There was a little pool of silence around them as they reached the dock—Race felt a little unsteady. The villagers were as unused to strangers as they, and stood a little off, staring. The man who had called approached them, speaking with a heartiness that did not cover his embarrassment. He held a tallysheet—a book of sheets an inch thick; tallyman or not, he was important.

"Don't let us bother you," said Janinda, perceiving this. "If you could tell us how to find the village. . . ."

"Out that door and up the bank," he said, becoming more embarrassed at her beauty. "They'll help you if you get lost."

The children followed her, looking down in confusion. Silence fell as they passed. Race glanced back as they went out the door, to see the steel teeth of the electric fork swing over with a ton and a half of hay, dropping it on a belt that carried it swiftly upward.

The harbor pool was at the bottom of a bowl, set back toward the top, with the north side much higher than the south. Broad stairs led from level to level, and small flowering trees held the banks in place. At the top of the north side they found themselves on level with the top of the dam. To the south the hill fell steeply to the plain, the gentle green sweep of which began immediately below and continued over the distant horizon. They had never looked down from such a height. They had never really seen the Plantation before.

Quite a number of villages clustered here; the farming villages that tilled the plain were distantly visible, there were two shipping villages at the canal head, and there appeared to be two or three more here atop the plateau—all within an hour's walk.

Turning their backs on the plain, they faced the mountain. It rose less than an hour's walk to the north and soared up literally into the sky—a haze of white hid its even whiter top. The break between plain and mountain was as sharp as a knife. Knowing nothing of mountains, the Wordens did not miss the foothills. The Oroné had flattened the higher hills into tablelands separated by the pools of the reservoirs; the lower hills had been cut off level with the plain and the bedrock pulverized, the gravel and sand spread over a dozen miles of plain, broken down now into black earth.

Word had spread ahead of them, and several hurrying men approached. "Welcome, ma'am, welcome to Waterton! It's a pleasure, a great pleasure—"

He was a paunchy sort with a ponderous air, with a balding head and a fur-trimmed jacket from which dangled the bronze keys of Authority. His face was full, round, and pale. He bobbed over Janinda's hand, then over Joss's, gave Race a brief shake, babbling names that none of them caught. The other men bobbed and grinned speechlessly. These were all village officials and Race became as shy as they; it amazed him that such important men should be so impressed by his mother, let alone himself. Their reputations were left far behind.

Janinda gave their first names and a false last name: Aram. "We're from Fulvia at the mouth of the canal, and we've always wanted to see the mountains—"

They broke in with praise of the mountains and it was unnecessary to say more for some time. None of these men could believe that anyone could live so far from the hills as did most plainsmen. They were deluged with invitations to stay at various houses. It was generally assumed that they intended to stay one night and return the next day, that Janinda's husband worked for the Transport Company and could not afford to take the day off for fear of losing his job, but that he could afford to send them. (Meaning that Janinda's job, if she held one, was not all that important to them.) The barges ran seven days a week, though the men worked but six.

The villagers were even more anxious to tell about themselves than to find out about strangers, and they managed to spend the rest of the afternoon without revealing much. Janinda did have to break their assumption, convenient though it was for them: she explained that they had heard that gold was to be found in the mountains, and that they hoped to be allowed to go seeking it.

A silence fell and the mountain men glanced at each other. "Well, ma'am, it's true. There's gold there if you can find it. But, well, that's apt to take months—even years—of steady searching, and the amount you come by in the process, hardly worth it."

"But there's no rule against it?"

"No, ma'am, so long as your job isn't neglected and you don't damage the Company or the Plantation, *they* don't care. And we don't either, of course.

"The mountains aren't safe, for all that. You know *they* have their Spires here in the hills, and they don't like people snooping around, it's said—"

"Near here?"

"No, ma'am, always to the south, mostly. I hear tell there's more far away up north"—indicating the southeast and northwest, respectively.

"Then there shouldn't be much danger."

"There's wild men and wild animals, ma'am, and the dangers of the mountains themselves—"

"Wild men?"

"Crazy men, ma'am, who ran away from the villages hereabouts. Almost every year we hear of one. God knows what they do, how they live. Anybody that would run away from the villages *must* be crazy."

Janinda compressed her lips. "Do they give you any trouble?"

"Us? No, ma'am. But we only go into the hills in large groups, woodcutting in winter, mostly." The Plantation built its own hay barges, and the mountains shipped wood to the plains. "And hunting, too."

"We have a rifle, and Race knows how to use it. There are animals we can eat?"

"Oh, yes, ma'am, more than on the plains. You're really determined? What about winter weather?"

"If we're going to find gold, we'll have it by that time. Whether or not, we'll come down and return to our jobs—unless we can get jobs here along the mountains." The men of Waterton sighed in relief.

3

General attitude was that the Wordens were mildly touched. Some of the younger villagers admired them, but most reflected the comfortable mental sloth of the plains villagers. It was as oppressive a feeling here, where men hunted and climbed the mountains for wood, as in the middle of the plain.

The men of Waterton led them to the store, and one went importantly behind the counter. "If you wish to seek for gold—we can be of little help there. Who knows what gold looks like in the ore?"

None did, but there was a good deal of advice tendered as to the washing of gold, which was an occasional pastime. They were instructed to buy a plastic household pan, quite shallow—Janinda bought two, they were quite cheap—and in a babble of voices they were told how to use it.

"You will require blankets and bedding." They had sufficient even for the frosty spring. "Good. Then you will wish one of our hunters' and woodcutters' tents." He lifted the corner of one, cunningly folded into a tiny pack. "These are made of woven sarth fur, covered with the sap of the rubba plant, which was then vulcanized. They are wind and waterproof, nearly as tough as tarpaulin, and nearly as light as silk."

They were expensive, but Janinda was only surprised that they were not more so. She bought one, her fine brow wrinkling. "We will also need shovels and hoes," she said in her quiet voice. "It was our thought to stay at one place and cast about for gold, and we could plant a garden."

"You seem not to care overmuch whether you find gold or not," observed the storekeeper. "Wise—and doubtless you'll enjoy yourselves among our little hills this fine summer. Shovels—and hoes—and, yes, a pick wouldn't be amiss. Well now, such things are not sold in any store that ever I heard of."

They were used in the communal gardens; the villages always sent for what was needed and paid a nominal sum out of their small treasuries.

"Maybe the village will sell ye such."

This produced an argument—Race groaned silently when he saw how the elders looked around for comfortable seats. Did the garden tools belong to the village, or to the Plantation? In the latter case they had no right to sell them and might be fired if some far-distant Accountant found against them, examining their records at Plantcontrol. Being fired was equivalent to being shot at dawn.

There was no *rule* against selling off the hand tools. Finally the representative of the Plantation, the Village Subsection Supervisor, was induced to go to his office and examine his records. They all trailed along. Puffing importantly, the Super opened his office, unlocked the computer link, and consulted his lists of parts.

"Garden hand tools are definitely not to be found in the Plantation lists," he said at length, importantly. "Under *any* cross-reference."

Turning to the Stores list, he quickly found them. This was the list of articles that could be bought to be sold in the stores—cooking utensils, cloth and clothing, even food.

Closing and locking his computer link, the Super turned impressively toward them. "That is definite—garden tools are private property, and ours belong to the village—*not* to the Plantation."

This posed a pretty problem for the village authorities. They debated it going back to the store. Should they sell one each of their tools? What price should be charged? What would be fair? How much would it cost to replace them?

At length, after the storekeeper had again unlocked his store and they were all settled comfortably, the Plantation Super—left out of the argument—re-injected himself.

"What becomes of the village's worn-out tools?"

They all knew that—they were taken to the metal-working shops to be used in welding and the like.

Janinda had used the occasion to buy the remaining small articles she lacked from the storekeeper; they were willing then to accompany the party to the nearest smithy. Here one of the men solemnly unlocked the door—it was still Sunday, rather to Race's surprise—and led them into his domain. This was Plantation property, and now a question arose. To whom did the scrap iron belong?

The village owned the tools—that was agreed. The worn-out tools were returned to the local representative of the Plantation. Did they then become Plantation property? Would the Plantation sell them, if so?

For quite ten minutes the village and the Plantation each disowned the tools. The village claimed no scrap iron on its lists; the Plantation had not paid for the tools. Janinda broke the deadlock: "Let each of you lay claim to them, then each renounce his claim, so that we will be in the clear either way. The computers do not keep track of such small details."

Whoever was responsible for the tools—or scrap—could be called to account for them—*they* were not in the clear. But her last sentence persuaded them—Plantation Control would never know.

It was done—and a new question arose. What should they charge her for them? Race's legs ached and his eyes were gritty with tiredness before they agreed that though the tools or scrap—Village and Plantation persisted in their own designations—though they had *use*, they had no *value* that could be calculated or written down. The Wordens could have them for nothing. It had taken well over an hour.

Joss whispered to Race, "Never mind, we've got lots more time than money."

The largest transaction was to come: they would need a beast of burden. Here at the foot of the mountains were huge barns full of various animals, all belonging to the Plantation. But over the decades animals had escaped—sickly ones certain to die, from which the Plantation relinquished its claim, but nursed back to health by some dedicated or ambitious admirer. Quite a herd of various useful animals had been accumulated, and were as carefully bred and cared for as the Plantation's, in barns as good as the Plantation's own. These animals they used on their unregulated hunts, and often when working for the Plantation, chiefly in woodcutting.

After much negotiating Janinda bought an old, very docile, but still sturdy bicaud from the village. That nearly exhausted her slender funds; she had not dreamed of the existence of draft animals.

The sun was only just setting, though darkness was a black-green velvet mist over the Plantation below. They accompanied the Subsection Supervisor home for the night, Race and even Joss uneasy at associating with such a great man. The Super at home was their Great-uncle Hale, who had no use for them. At least, the houses of the Supers were no bigger or better than the rest.

Under his air of ponderous authority the Super was as ignorant and curious as a child. Race found himself a little shocked to realize that the Authorities of Waterton and Ravenham were equally ignorant and closed of mind. Their adventures had already begun to change him. The Super, like most village elders, preferred to expound his wisdom rather than to learn. He talked heavily of the mountains, woodcutting, hunting (frivolous pursuits he had rarely followed), and even a few nuggets on gold-washing. Perhaps as many as ten stars were washed yearly by the inhabitants of Waterton.

It sounded like a lot at first. A star was a ten-gram coin, one silver star being four days' average wages in the Plantation. In her years of saving, Janinda had accumulated nine silver stars and as much more in half-stars and copper tenths. But there were several hundred inhabitants of Waterton, and since a gold star was worth only ten silver stars, it came to about a day's wage per person per year.

Race shared a bedroom under the eaves with the Super's youngest son, a ten-year-old called How. The lad was immeasurably excited by his visitor from the rim of the world and kept him awake for hours, questioning him about Fulvia and life on the main canal, where the barge trains ran all night long. Head spinning with the varied images of the day, Race answered as best as he could.

How said, "When I grow up I'm going to go to Fulvia and get a job with the Company, running to Plantation Control and the locks!" To him, the mountains were as dull as the plains to Race.

Race awoke confused next morning, thinking it winter and time to get up for school, but the gongs of the locomotives started strange half-dreams drifting through his mind. On awakening fully, he thrilled from head to foot: the barge trains were making up and pulling out to the south, and the cold air was flowing down from the mountains. He shivered in the predawn, careful not to wake How.

But the boy woke anyway. It being Monday, he had to get ready for school and had little time for questions. The Super's wife, a plump, super-respectable sort who oppressed her sons, set out an early breakfast for them. Clearly she did not know whether to be glad that their disturbing presence would soon be gone, or alarmed that others might follow their mad example.

The Super's presence at the Offices was not so pressing that he had no time to see them off. Quite a number of the village authorities turned out to see them, even helping to carry their belongings to the village barns where the stable-hands showed them how to pack their bicaud.

They were fearful of the beast. It stood a little less high than Race's shoulder at its front shoulder. Its front legs were longer than its back ones and its spine extended from the tip of its tail forward in a sweeping bowl-curve over the front shoulder and down over the top of the skull, terminating in a prehensile front tail about a foot and a half long. The nostril opened immediately under this foretail, and the under side of it was pink and fleshy, the scent-organ surface extending along it.

The head under its spine was long and narrow, bulging aft. Large mild eyes on opposite sides of the head had disconcerting horizontal pupils, thin jet slits that made Race and Joss nervous. Some breeds, they knew, had a pair of spines protruding from the head or nose in the females. Theirs was a gelded male or *gent*.

The villagers called them, familiarly, "byes". Bicauds were covered with horny scutes like those of a turtle but big as a man's palm, five or six sided. They were transparent but usually amber or olive tinted; they could be peeled off without too much pain to the animal, which promptly grew new ones if too many hadn't been taken at once. Polished and set on wood or leather or glass, they were popular ornaments even in the villages. Race's father had been burned in a bicaud belt.

"Goodbye!" "Goodbye!" "Good luck!" "Good hunting!" "We'll see you next fall!" "Look out for the wild men!"

The Wordens waved back and set out eagerly. It was about sunup. To their left was the deep arm of the reservoir that reached down to the dam, no wider than the canal below; the reservoir was well to their left ahead, hidden behind trees. The hard-packed road was already full of tractors that never saw a plow, pulling loads of hay toward the barns.

From the village to the abrupt sweep of the mountain, the tableland was covered with clusters of barns amid clusters of trees, huge barns, sprawling barns. An amazing mingling of early morning noises came from them, along with a dry, musty odor that they had noticed in the village. There were many more animals than people here—tons of animals for every human. Most ate grass products; some of the fur-bearers ate the offal of the slaughterhouses. For more than an hour they trod the road, waving at the tractor Operators and looking nervously at the bye as it walked with them.

It took no notice of the tractors. They had been instructed to walk beside its head at all times, on the downhill side, gripping the foretail lightly as a lead. It plodded sturdily along, a little slower than they were used to, shedding a strong, pleasant animal odor. It never made a sound.

The road rose gradually, then progressively more steeply, turning to the right, away from the reservoir. Presently it came to the back of the tableland, where the slope was covered with a dense tangle of trees against erosion. Here, the road made one meander before plunging out of sight. The Wordens didn't think to look back. They were beyond civilization now, the road showing only a few tracks and an occasional animal dropping.

"Did he tell you?" Joss asked of their mother.

Janinda's voice was lower than usual, though no one could have heard them. "The stablehand? Yes—he said to turn right at the first road after the Split Rock. But I couldn't understand why."

A stablehand, unusually silent in the presence of the village authorities, had found occasion to murmur to Race and Joss.

"That road will take us south to a different valley, south of the mountain. It's narrower, but there's a pass at the back that will lead us through the mountains to the plain on the other side."

For a while nobody said anything. Then Janinda sighed. "I was hoping no one would realize we intend to go through; they'd have thought we were crazy. Apparently it happens pretty often—whether the elders know it or not."

"So you don't expect to see any wild men?" Joss seemed a little disappointed.

"I don't know. I can't imagine why they'd stay in the mountains."

The road turned to their left again and definitely descended. They kept expecting it to debouch into a clearing, being unused to and rather fearful of forests. But though they got glimpses of an open space, probably the reservoir, and passed through thinned areas where trees had been cut, they never saw the big glade. At Split Rock, a huge, broken boulder, they had a glimpse of the broad, pleasant valley down which the canal's waters came.

Here, they turned right onto a narrow road in which occasional plants grew. Race was bemused at the numerous broad-leafed plants. It led steeply uphill. Janinda fell behind, to press out the marks of the bicaud's claws and once shoveling droppings off the road. "To keep people from following us and dropping in for a visit," she said.

They had heard occasional tractors and voices and the ring of an axe, but as they mounted the shoulder, those noises fell away. Atop the shoulder they were between a steep hill and the mountain proper; farther on, the road descended, then swung over to perch precariously on the flank of the mountain.

Here they were among pine trees, the first they had seen. Joss plucked handfuls of the needles and bark, sniffing at them. Waterton was now out of sight beyond the shoulder behind them, but they had occasional glimpses of the plains. About noon the road trended definitely upward, here little more than a track which no tractor had ever seen. It was slanting away to the left, they decided, and concluded that they were gradually drawing into the mouth of the valley.

They stopped to eat a little before noon, in a glade that gave them a broad view of the plains—the first they'd had. And, they realized, the last they'd have. They stared south. The plains were a rich kelly green with forest green dots. None doubted that Ravenham was on the horizon, and they strained their eyes to see it. Strange feelings went through Race. He had never imagined distance or altitude that could reduce Ravenham to a dark green dot on the edge of vision. Could they even see it from here?

Actually, it stood well above the horizon. The horizon was all of sixty miles away from this altitude, and Ravenham but thirty. The faint dark line that seemed to bound the earth was the line of hills on the far side of the Plantation. They were looking far over the head of Ravenham.

It was hot in the sunshine and they plunged into the shade gratefully. All were silent, long after they turned their backs on the plains. They were definitely in a valley; they saw the mountaintop to the south crowding in over them. The mountains seemed to shut together ahead, but as they plodded on that day, each turn still revealed a narrow trail.

They were very tired when they camped that night. Since the road stayed near the bottom of the valley, there was water, icy cold, from the loud stream. It was not necessary to stake out the *gent*. They made the mistake of cooking and eating supper first, and when they started to pitch their tent it was getting dark. After a struggle that made Race mad and Joss laugh, they gave up.

"If it rains, we can spread it over us like a tarp," said Janinda.

Joss approached Race's bed in the chill dusk. "Race? Mom told me ... about the flagstone. Oh, Race, did you really lift it?"

He felt uncomfortable; her tone was eager, almost worshipful. Come to think of it, there had been a shortage of sharp sisterly comments while setting up camp.

"It raised up, is all I know."

"Oh, *Race*! Think of it! Isn't it wonderful?"

"Yeah."

"How big a thing can you lift? Can you fly, like one of *them*?"

"I don't know what I can do. I haven't tried anything."

She stared at him, eyes big in the dimness. "Haven't tried! Race Worden! If I had done something like that I wouldn't have slept before—you're not kidding? Are you afraid?"

It was difficult to explain to a girl, especially your sister just into her teens, he found. "I don't know exactly how I did it ... and there's not been time to think," he said lamely.

He *was* afraid. His whole world had gone topsy-turvy in an instant. Remembered chills went through him. In the days since, he had managed to forget the immediacy of that feeling; now it came back to him with full force. It amazed him that he could virtually have forgotten the incident for two whole days.

But there would be time enough to think about it when they reached the mountains ... years in the future. Now, here they were. Now he *had* to think of it.

When he developed full Starling abilities (if he could), he'd have to confront a Starling ... sooner or later. *Hello, sir. How do you do? I'm a Starling, too. Watch this!* He shuddered.

"Mom wants to get farther away from the plains. They sometimes go on three or four day hunting trips, and we're only one day from Waterton—closer to some of the other villages."

"Can't you just pick us all up and fly us over the mountain?"

Race became conscious again of the ache in his legs. He grunted. "I wish I could!" For the first time he looked more kindly on his possible Starling powers.

4

It was a long chilly night. Race lay awake for hours, breathing in the cold piny air and listening to the murmurs of his mother and sister; the hoots and calls of unfamiliar night birds, the chirrings of familiar bugs, and the sound of the stream filling the night air with moisture.

The ground was hard and rough under his blankets. He tossed and turned.

Could he really, after all, develop full Starling powers? Who ever heard of a human becoming a Starling, outside of a fairy story? Just what powers were these?

Starlings could fly through the air—everybody knew that. They could move other things with the power of their minds, size no limit. Mountains definitely, planets most likely. There was hardly an inhabited planet in the Galaxy that had not had its orbit trimmed ... but Race knew little history and that was merely a rumor. He put it down as doubtful.

It was said that Starlings were healers without parallel, that they themselves never died, that they lived a very, very long time, or that they lived several times as long as humans. It was said that they did not talk at all; that they could talk mind to mind, without sound, that they could talk thus over long distances. It was said that they could sense, see, and/or hear things at a distance, anywhere on the planet, or on planets of nearby stars. It was said that they could manufacture living beings in any size or shape, plant or animal; that

even the human race was their creation, God having
created only Starlings "in His image". It was said that
they could make gold and silver out of stone or lead or
nothing; that they flew out into space and found as-
teroids of solid gold and silver, or mountains of metals
on planets with pisonous air. It was said that when
they died, they were reborn immediately as Starling babies; that they could talk to the spirits of the departed
and that they could send their souls out of their bodies
into the land of departed spirits. It was said that they
flew regularly to Heaven and that they were angels sent
to rule men for their own good; that they were saintly
men who were promoted to angelic status; that they
were descendants of Jesus, the Son of God.

It was said . . . it was said. . . .

Race was a young, ignorant peasant. The credulous
peasants had open-mindedly accepted all of these tales,
with the reservation that Starlings were unknown and
unknowable by ordinary sinful men. Any stories not
literally true were figuratively so. The many culture-
hero myths that told about Starlings required accepting
different origins or powers. But who could deny that
Starlings could do this or that? Better to believe and
enjoy the story.

But listing them all at once was too much, even for
Race's untrained critical faculties. Surely they couldn't
all be true.

It was generally agreed, mentioned casually in the
schoolbooks (supplied by *them,* and surely *they* knew),
that men and Starlings once inhabited Old Earth. Starlings won the stars (whence their name), and carried
men with them to the planets. All this hundreds of
years ago. Mavia was settled from Sonissa about the
time of the break-up of the Hundred-Star Crown—the
Imperial Cluster blazed, a fierce hazy ball, over his
head now. That would be about two hundred years
ago. Sonissa and Mavia were then in the Seventeen-Star
Crown of the Rosemonts of Neolan.

Actually—here the schoolbooks were explicit—there

were never more than sixteen stars ruled by the Rosemonts, Neolan and Elysia orbiting the same star. The Rosemont Crown quickly broke up, Sonissa and its colony Mavia among the first to break away; currently the Rosemonts ruled about two planets and a single star. Mavia was now independent of, but friendly with, Sonissa.

The Imperial Cluster was a galactic cluster of average size—about five hundred stars in a space thirty light years across. It now had a hundred inhabited planets, after terraformation. The many doublets and triplets reduced the number of actual stars in the crown to about seventy, though there were dozens of mining and military outposts on uninhabited stars.

Beyond it lay the unknown. The Imperial Cluster had absorbed the energies of the expanding Starling wave in this direction. Now it was occupied by forty more or less independent provinces split into assorted factions, all giving lip-service to the ideal of unity.

Mavia looked on it with suspicion; the cluster had been expansionistic just before break-up, and Mavia was originally a military settlement.

That was the actual extent of Race's historical knowledge. This was elaborated somewhat by the name of various rulers and generals, dates and places of occasional battles between Starlings. Of actual Starling powers the books mentioned only one, their power of flight. (Race had no concept of the distances between stars and was not aware that light had a velocity; starflight and flight through the air were the same to him.) Two, their ability to move masses from small to very large size by mind. Three, the ability to sense the location and composition of masses of matter, as buried ore. That was all.

The thought cheered him. He would not have to learn to handle the godlike powers of healing and mental communication (to say nothing of flights to Heaven. How could he confront God, if he shied at the thought of meeting a Starling?).

Race had not spent ten years, six days a week or three in hoeing seasons, in accumulating the above meager facts. Much of his time between the ages of five and fifteen had been spent in the study of technology and various useful skills, such as rough-and-ready first aid. He understood the operation of the geothermal power plants that drove the barge locomotives and heated Ravenham's houses; knew how to wind a motor or generator and could quickly have picked up the skills of an electrotechnician, having all the basics. He understood the Gas Laws and the theory of steam power, could troubleshoot a steam tractor, and quickly could have learned to repair them. He knew the basics of metallurgy and could have been accepted as an apprentice in any welding shop. He understood the germ theory of disease and knew the value of sanitation and cleanliness; also he knew the elements of nutrition. He knew about radio waves, satellite relays, and had read of television, but here his understanding was limited. The Plantation communicated with the villages by cable. He knew of computers and had a vague idea of how they worked.

Race and his fellow peasants had a better grasp of the basic technology of their society than had the much better-educated people of the higher technological civilization which spawned the Starlings. But this was mostly from books; Race had never seen a radio, nor heard a voice electronically reproduced or transmitted. Nor had he ever seen a microscope, telescope, a doorbell, or a hot-water faucet.

Race shifted, noting again the ache in his legs. So much walking, all uphill, had been too much even for the Wordens, who expected to walk anywhere. "Can't you just fly us over the mountain?" Joss had asked. *If only. . . .*

Well, why not? He *had* moved the flagstone—he thought. Race stared at a long-fingered pine branch silhouetted against the Imperial Cluster, unconsciously tensing all his muscles and holding his breath in the intensity of his concentration, willing himself up, willing the branch to grow larger against the pale flaming sky. . . .

With a gasp he relaxed. Despite his utmost concentration, he had been conscious of the rocks poking through the blankets under him throughout. Race felt like a fool.

They were all as stiff as boards next morning, between the unaccustomed chill and the weariness of the day before. "It will get colder as we go higher," Joss reminded them, hopping from foot to foot before the fire.

"We will have to find more food today," said Janinda, her expression as calm as ever despite the smoke in her eyes. Except at picnics on the edge of the fields they never saw fire. "Joss, you and I had better lead the bye while Race carries the rifle and goes ahead, or to one side."

Race expected Joss to object that she could shoot as well as he, which she firmly believed. But she had become attached to their bicaud, which she had named Nod. Race fetched the rifle and was tempted to warm it at the fire, but that would provoke a "funny" remark from his dear little sister. He laid it on a stump facing the sun.

They had woken late, though the sun had not yet risen. Here in the mountains the sky was a deeper color, almost blue at the zenith. The apple-green color seemed wonderfully transparent, as if one could sink thousands of miles into the sky. There were more clouds than usual, flushing the usual deep rose at dawn.

"I never knew how hungry cold air could make you," said Race gloomily, observing the small portions Janinda was dishing out. Her thick soup was sustaining but she held out half of it for the next meal. "I hope our bullets will last the summer."

"They should see us through the mountains. I wonder what kinds of jobs are to be found over there, and if there's much competition for them."

Joss looked at Janinda and Race but said nothing.

"Maybe we'll have a fistful of gold to sell."

"We can't bank on it."

They had less than one star remaining. A large box of shells cost just one silver star.

"I've been thinking," said Joss unexpectedly.

"Wow!"

She flushed and stuck out her tongue at him. "Remember what the Super said in Waterton—that they washed ten stars of gold a year? Well, ten gold stars is a hundred or a hundred and twenty silver stars—the value of gold has been going up the past few years. That's about half a silver star for every working man or woman in Ravenham—and Waterton is about the same size. Now, they don't all go out and wash gold. Only a few do, mostly in winter when they're supposed to be cutting wood. And they can't work at it constantly. So there must be quite a bit of gold about. If we work at it all summer—"

"It does sound promising," Janinda admitted.

"I wonder if those crazy men they told us about didn't stumble on quite a lot of gold at once—"

"A big pocket."

"Yes. A big pocket, and decided to run away over the mountains, like us? These mountain men have a lot more freedom and opportunities than we ever did, even if they do have to work hard all winter."

"That all sounds reasonable," Janinda said.

Joss smiled at her. "Now it's your turn! What have you been thinking about?"

Janinda laughed with them and tossed her hair back in her characteristic manner—Race had once seen his sister practicing it. "I *have* been wondering about food plants. Do the kinds we're familiar with, growing wild, grow this far up?"

"A good question—it'll be months before that famous garden of ours produces any food. There are lots of broad-leaved plants here."

"We'll all have to watch."

A squirn ran out on a limb and chattered and scolded them, flirting its fluffy tail. They were found in every village, half-tame, and the Wordens would no more have dreamed of eating one than of eating dogs or cats.

This day's climb was as long as the previous one, and took them past the two mountains they had camped between. The stream fell down in foam, over the face of the pass between them. The road branched every which way here. They followed a faint trace up the steep slope, always staying close to the water. The bye, Nod, waded stolidly through an icy tributary over which they had to leap, undignified.

Nod did not have to be tied, staked, or hobbled at night. He hung about, and anytime they awoke they could hear him stuffing leaves or grass into his mouth with his foretail, or the peculiar gurgle of his digestive system.

Once beyond the first two mountains they found they had merely graduated from kindergarten. They were in a high valley between two *real* mountains, with treeless, snow-covered tops. It had not really occurred to any of them that a chain of mountains could be more than one mountain thick. Beyond, they could see still more white tops.

Joss pointed to the most distant one. "What do you bet that one's farther from the edge of the plains than Ravenham?"

It was a sobering thought.

"You were the one who objected to the garden idea," Race told her. "Do you still feel like just traveling around?"

She grinned sheepishly and rubbed her leg. "I don't *feel* like it, but I *do* want to see the mountains." She looked eagerly around at their up-and-down horizon.

Janinda led them on, her quiet voice determined, until the peaks ahead of them thinned out and they occasionally descended slopes. Now they found that they were going downstream. They found that deer and other fairly large animals also lived in the mountains—more plentiful than in the plains—and were much less shy. They recognized numerous food plants and generally got on well enough, except for exhaustion, for a week.

"I should think we're far enough north not to be bothered by anyone," she finally said. "We must look out for a good garden site; the season's getting on, even here. And I wonder if we can't contrive some better shelter than this tent. . . ."

If Race had had full Starling powers, he could have carved a house out of stone in half a day. If!

Every night, and daily while ranging far from the bye with his rifle, Race tried to lift himself into the air. It always made him feel both foolish and mad. But the pain in his legs or the breath whistling through his lungs was always enough to make him try again. So far, without luck.

Picking a bench with a good outlook to the north, so that the sun might reach the seeds, they broke the thin harsh soil with the shovel, hoe and axe. The latter was essential; tree roots twined through it. They had never seen virgin soil before. "I never wished for a tractor so much," Race panted once. It was hot work.

Digging for gold, which they took up with considerable enthusiasm, was almost as hot and much more disappointing. Janinda preferred to stay near the garden plot, on which the animals would prey if not warded off.

Days, then weeks, trickled past. They erected a framework of saplings and stretched their tent over it. Race spent two days with the axe, cutting poles to lay across the south side, to keep out the wind-blown rain.

"Come winter, if we have to, we can put up four walls of poles and pile dirt up against them," he said, hoping it would never come to that.

Yet it might. They had found no gold, and while they got on well enough—though Janinda missed soap—they made no advances for a month. Race's half-hearted efforts to lift himself or some large animal he had shot became whole-hearted, to no avail.

Joss said nothing. The subject of his possible powers was never mentioned. Race himself never brought it up, and clearly Joss had been warned by their mother. Race sometimes noticed an intent look on her face and got the feeling that she and even his mother paid unusual attention to his comings and goings, to every word he spoke, to his moods. It made him uncomfortable. Though no powers were manifest, he was already being cut off from his kin and kind.

He did not spend all his time brooding. Once he came upon Joss with her head thrown back, face screwed up in her intensity of concentration, rising up on her tiptoes and falling back, every muscle tense. He managed to keep from laughing, and slunk silently away, not to embarrass her. For a week he was in a good mood—and tried conscientiously.

But during the second month he felt the pressure of time on him. The summer, short here in the mountains though they were nearer the equator, was passing, day by sun-shot day, and he had nothing to show for it. He became solitary and morose.

All of them had grown silent. The first excitement of the mountains had gone, nor was there the occasion for the incessant talk of village life. Janinda, never talkative, now rarely spoke. Otherwise she seemed not to have changed at all. Joss became greatly attached to Nod and spent much of her time holding his foretail and talking, or sprawling over his back and peering into his eyes. The bicaud never wandered far at night and drifted near toward dawn, to be found every morning beside her bed, rocking from foot to foot and gurgling internally. He only had to be scolded thrice by her for getting into the garden.

When not with the bye, Joss roamed the valley with a vacant look, humming, singing when she was too far away for the words to be distinguishable. Sometimes she carried the shovel and a pan, at others the axe.

One day, two months after they had arrived here, Race returned empty-handed from an all-day hunting trip. He had been brooding more than usual of late, paying no attention to game signs. He was tired, and wearily hated the mountains, where every step was either up or down hill and not even the bench was level. He had tried all day, persistently but without hope, to fly. Now he came trailing in through the rose and gold dusk, hot, tired, and sullen.

Crossing the stream below the bench and coming up it, he passed a broad shallow pool that was warmed daily by the sun. A movement caught his eye and he lifted the rifle automatically, peering through the spiny bushes.

Joss stood naked in the pool, half knee-deep, looking serenely up at the rose and gold of the sunset on the snow-clad peaks above them. She absently wiped excess water off her body, humming a quiet tune.

Race's throat hurt with the sight. Her small breasts were just the size to fit his palm; her brown legs were woman-shaped yet still girl-slim, while the line of her hip and the breadth of her flat arrowhead of an abdomen gave promise of future development equal to their mother's. Joss was becoming a young woman.

Well, of course! Race was of marriageable age this year, she was two years younger. He had never thought of Joss as anything but a girl. *Miss Jocela Worden. . . .*

After that first startled look he jerked his eyes away, guiltily, and climbed the bench looking at the sky. It was the first time that day Race had noticed the magnificence of the mountains; it had grown familiar. Now again it struck him, the heights, the wild shaggy sweeps, the wheeling birds, and the sunsets and dawns. Clouds were visible every day, now glowing gold high up, flushing pink low down, and throwing their colors on the blazing snowfields. Between the mountain tops and the clouds, the sky was a deep pure green.

At the camp Race grunted incoherently in reply to Janinda's serene greeting, caught up the axe, and plunged up the slope. Wood was not a pressing item, nor did he cut much. He stayed till it was too dark to see, then stumbled back with a meager armload, forgetting the axe.

Janinda, with her usual insight, had not troubled him with calls to supper. They had set his share back and it was still warm. Race ate it silently, conscious of their murmur of talk as he was of the stream's, but made uncomfortable by it. Immediately he went to bed. The nights were warm now, and Race was hot. He tossed and turned as if he had never gotten used to sleeping on a pallet, or they had never learned to cut leafy twigs to put under them.

It was not visions of Joss's serene nudity that troubled him, nor so much his guilt at having seen her. It was that he had failed them. Joss and his mother had taken this desperate chance in the hope that he could master his powers and pull them through. He had let them down.

Where could they go? What could they do? *Back to Ravenham?* He could say that he had *tried*. But he hadn't, not really. He had never gone into the thing, thought it out, *felt* his way down inside himself to see what feelings would govern the powers. Because, to move one's arm takes no concentration; merely a keying, directing emotion, a will or desire to move. Flying should be governed by a similar feeling.

He considered this for a long time with no effect, and found himself concentrating with straining muscles and clenched teeth in the old way he knew was hopeless. Race deliberately exhaled, letting his muscles go limp, on the verge of despair. If he had been much younger the tears would have come.

He turned over and looked dully up at the sky. The Imperial Cluster now rose less than an hour before sunset. It now blazed between two mountains to the northeast, yielding more light than the moon of any planet.

For a moment, Joss's serene beauty swam before him. Guiltily he jerked his mind away, and for a moment a kaleidoscope of Joss's face and voice in many moods over several years poured through his mind. Oddly, he found himself remembering her words about old Keithly, the night before their flight.

Race had almost forgotten the black-bearded foreman; he was little more than a name and a blurred face, no longer feared. Nor could he clearly recall his hours atop the tall tractor, sweeping through the green sea and turning it brown. But a little of the trapped, scared, hopeless feeling he had known on realizing that he would spend the rest of his life atop that tractor returned to him with the memory of Joss's words that night.

Underneath that fear was the hope that his lifting of the flagstone might win him free of Ravenham. That brought vividly to mind the actual lifting itself—the open half-door seemed so close he could touch it. For two months and more it had faded to nothing but a verbal description, but now the actual scene itself returned, not at all faded. The strange mingling of fear and amazement went through him again and turned his limbs to jelly.

Deliberately Race brought his mind back, again and again, to the actual instant of lifting and the few seconds before. There it all was: the recurrent irritation at the stone, driven by the indignity of splashing into a puddle (Joss had laughed); a feeling of *if only* and the usual impatient jerk of his mind—*it should be up here*—and a quivering tension.

This time, he recalled, he had not merely visualized where it should be, but actually its rising into position. And that quivering tension he had never felt before.

Concentrating, he built up the feeling—dropped it

when icy fingers plunged into his belly. For half a minute he wondered whether he had actually risen off the
pallet. With a sudden motion, Race threw off the cover
and reached for his pants.

5

At the edge of their garden was a large rock they had tried to remove. When they had dug down knee-deep and found that the rock was still wider, they had given up. Now it made a convenient place to sit.

His broad, vague shadow monstrous beside him, Race picked his way down the bench to the garden in the clusterlight. Crouching above the rock, he brought back the emotions of the flagstone-raising. The irritation he didn't need, but the strong impatient desire to *change* things he did, and the queer tension.

Remembering his irritation brought the other two back. As the tension grew in him, Race remembered that he must visualize the rock's rise. To do so he visualized it lying under the ground, and immediately realized his image was inaccurate. The stone was much wider below than at its top, and correspondingly thicker . . . and he found that it had an unexpected outthrust below ground. However, he managed to visualize this odd shape—his sudden sharp fear strengthened the tension—this odd shape *rising*—and with a faint sound the ground under his feet lifted. Choking with excitement and fear, Race backed up. The quivering went all through him now, but he didn't let his fear break the tension as it had before. The boulder had risen but a few inches. Now he brought it up farther. There was only the faint sound of earth falling in behind it . . . Race was conscious of making no more effort than is usually involved in manipulating mental images.

The boulder climbed a yard, six feet, eight feet. Clear of the hole, it hung while Race stared at it, panting with excitement and fear. He expected that any moment it would slip out of his grasp; the slightest break in his concentration and he would lose it, and he had an almost overwhelming desire to look behind him.

With an effort he caused it to move toward him, stumbling back out of its way, and he stopped it over the ground beyond the garden. He had to force it down as he had raised it up; no amount of relaxing caused it to fall. Only the effort of concentration was needed to support it, as if it had no weight . . . once down on the ground Race had difficulty in letting go of it. It took an effort like waking up to break his concentration.

Released, the boulder—and now he realized how huge it was—promptly turned over, turned again, then rolled down to the garden and out a little way. Race's frantic effort to lift or stop it had no effect; it was changing position too rapidly for him to visualize. Then it was still and he could sit down. His legs quivered from strain.

"Oh, Race, Race, Race! You *did* it! Oh, Race!"

Joss flung herself on him incoherently, hugging him and kissing his startled face, babbling, oblivious of her short nightgown. Janinda, wearing her housecoat, knelt beside him to throw one arm around him. All three stared deliriously at the great rock.

"So you've figured it out, Race!" said Janinda. "I was sure you would."

"It wasn't easy!" A sigh that was half a groan.

"Poor Race! I'm sure it wasn't. I would have given anything if I could have helped."

"How did you do it? It looked so easy! Was it hard?"

"It is easy. They only hard thing is the concentration." The logjam broke and Race spoke more easily than he had in two months. It all came out, including his fears that they'd have to go back to Ravenham, except Joss's part. They listened, Janinda content, Joss intent.

"Do you mean to say you saw that knob on the side while the rock was still underground?"

Race was startled. "Why . . . I just knew it had that shape. I didn't really see it, I just visualized it. Look at that tree, then close your eyes and bring it back and you'll know what I mean. It was so natural that I never realized it."

Joss looked at the rock and closed her eyes tightly, but nothing happened. Disappointed, she opened them and said, "Do it again!"

Race quivered and Janinda said gently, "I think Race has done enough for tonight. He seems completely exhausted."

Joss sprawled in a graceful tangle of limbs across his lap. For a moment her face was very girlish and quite sullen with disappointment. Race had a flash image of himself unable to move the rock in the morning.

"Maybe I'd better get in a little more practice," he said hastily. With both of them breathing at his ear he had a harder time bringing up the peculiar tension, but after a prolonged moment he felt it growing. His old image of the boulder was no longer accurate; now it lay on its side. He visualized it in that attitude and felt his image altering, the details on the far side coming into focus as his strange perceptive power began to operate.

"I'm going to take it straight up about three or four feet," he whispered, tensely, and did so with an effort. He concentrated more fiercely than perhaps was necessary. Joss frowned and squinted at the boulder also, and even Janinda looked intently at it.

When he had it up high enough he had a little trouble; he kept trying to visualize it right side up. They all gasped as it began to rotate in midair; Race had not consciously visualized it turning top side up. He felt more comfortable when it stopped turning, but his control and concentration hadn't wavered, as he had feared they would.

He moved it through the air to a point farther away than its first stopping point, and brought it down until its bottom touched the ground again. Now he stared at it unhappily. This was a flatter place, but it still might roll—the thing was dangerously big. After several seconds, he simply forced it down into the ground.

It sank in, came to a stop, then in further and stopped. There was no more effort in moving it through earth than through air, but he felt it natural for a push to send it only so far into the ground. Realizing his error he moved it smoothly down to a depth of three feet, and after a little hesitation released it. He half expected the compressed earth to hurl it out again, but it merely quivered and tipped a little, rising an inch at one corner.

Joss kissed him again. He was less weak this time. "I don't think I'll need any more practice."

Race lay awake long, for an hour hearing the excited murmurs of Joss and the soothing replies of his mother. He never knew when he went to sleep, but awakened once gripping the distant boulder with his mind—he had dreamed that it had started to roll. He had to wake all the way up to release it, but promptly fell into leaden sleep again.

Sunlight in his eyes awoke him. The sun was peering over the shoulder of the mountain to the northeast and he had overslept by two hours. The odor of frying meat came to him and he saw Joss climbing up on the boulder. Race dressed hastily while her back was turned and hurried down to the stream to wash.

Joss joined him and he realized that they had overslept by at least an hour themselves.

"Can you still do it? You haven't forgotten?"

Race wiped cold water from his face. "Sure." He hadn't the slightest doubt, though in the bright sunlight last night's silver-and-ink escapade seemed like a dream.

"Do something! Can you fly? Fly us back to the fire!"

Race caught her excitement. "I'll try."

With her staring into his eyes he found it difficult to concentrate, but by looking past her and half closing them he managed, after quite awhile, to bring back the tension. Then he lifted himself, like standing up. It was that automatic, and much easier, involving no muscular effort.

"Oooh! Oh, Race!" Joss was almost whispering in rapture.

He moved himself back down—he had only lifted a couple of feet—and took her hand. Confidently he rose, until dragged down by her hand. Frowning he looked down into her anxious face, concentrated on her, nearly fell out of the air, and was suddenly conscious of the sweet slight form under her pants and shirt.

"I've got to do a little practice," he said hastily, ears red. Letting go, he moved himself smoothly and confidently across the stream, around a tree; he swung himself horizontal and looped it again to return to her side.

"I've got it!"

Personal flight was automatic; but to move some other body, flesh or stone, required concentration on its form. His brief flight was all the practice he needed for himself. Now concentrating on her slim hourglass form did not cause him to lose himself. Joss grabbed frantically for his hand as he lifted her up to him, and threw her head back ecstatically.

"Up, up!"

Race lifted them into the air along a steep slope like the rise of a bicaud's back, upright but head a little in advance of feet. At the top of the slope he brought their feet forward, his own easily first, hers a bit clumsily next, and they slid down the air to land lightly just before the fire. They automatically bent their knees to take the shock—they came in pretty fast—but Race had instantly halted them on touching ground.

Janinda looked up just in time to see their approach.

She laughed with them, seeming not at all surprised, to Joss's disappointment.

"Hunting won't be so hard now," she said. "And poor Nod won't have to carry the big ones back."

"Hey, yeah!" Race hadn't had time to think of that.

"Can I come with you?" Joss bounced with eagerness.

"I guess. If you don't squeal and scare all the game. We better go this morning, too; I didn't get anything yesterday."

"Come with us, Mom? It's wonderful! Show her, Race!"

Joss turned to him with both hands outstretched. Unhesitatingly, Race caught her hands and visualized her trim hips, then lifted. Holding her down by her hands caused her to go up like a bent jackknife, head and feet hanging down, until she gave a sudden ecstatic kick that placed her standing on her head in his mental grasp. He dropped her quickly to the ground.

"Just like a tumbling act at Fulvia!" said Janinda, laughing with them. She dished up their breakfasts, saying, "Perhaps I shall come with you. It must be wonderful. And I haven't been far from the camp this month."

"I've always wanted to go up that spur up there, but it's too far to walk. Or up to the snow line! Wouldn't that be wonderful on a hot day? Can we go over to the next valley to the south and see what's there?"

"We'll go all over," Race said between bites. "It's a long time before winter."

Janinda cleared her throat. "You said last night that you sensed or saw the shape of the boulder while it was underground. Can you really see things behind you, or far away, or underground?"

Race frowned in thought. He had been conscious of the tree that made one post of their shelter, standing behind him. But he had seen it before he sat down. Now that he concentrated on it, though, details of branch stubs and limbs came to him of which he wouldn't have been conscious normally. Concentrating on the ground below him, he was vaguely aware that there was a large stone to one side; a mere dark mass.

"Not very far away. And it's not really like seeing, like I told you—".

"No doubt you'll get better. Can you tell the difference between, oh, a rock and a piece of wood?"

"Of course!" The roots of the tree were obvious—much lighter in feel than the stones.

"How about different kinds of rocks?"

That was right, Starlings could locate ore just by flying over it. He concentrated, said, "I guess I'm not that good yet."

"But what makes the difference between rocks and wood, and rocks and rocks, if they're underground where you can't see the color?" Joss asked.

"The weight. You can tell by the feel how heavy they are, for their size."

"So it should be possible to tell one rock from another? Gold," said Janinda thoughtfully, "is just about the densest metal anyone ever heard of."

Joss and Race stared at her. Disappointment had long since killed their dreams of gold. "Do you really think—"

"Why not? We know there's gold here, from the men of Waterton. We know Starlings can locate ores—learned that in school. And we know you can sense such things. Doubtless you just need practice."

Joss stared at him wide-eyed, realizing for the first time that he was, must be, a *Starling*. "Do you really think you can do all those things—you know—"

Race shook his head sharply. "I don't know what I can do, or Starlings can. But I do know that the schoolbooks only mention three things for sure: flying, moving things, and 'sensing'. You remember the history book said that Wilimer Rosemont 'sensed' the presence of a large bed of uranium ore on Sonissa. Apparently that's what they call it."

"Then you can't heal people, say, or turn stone to water or that kind of thing?"

Race shook his head again and Janinda spoke. "It stands to reason that there must be limits to Starling powers, else they wouldn't need humans. Who grows their grass for them, raises their cattle—even transports freight from place to place, which they could do better and faster?"

His mother seemed not at all disconcerted that he was a Starling. Race was. It was true, it really was. A *Starling*. For a moment he felt alone and very cold in the early sunlight, his belly empty as if he hadn't just finished a good breakfast.

But Joss was there. She sat leaning back, her eyes screwed up in thought, smiling to herself. She said, "I was just thinking about Ravenham. What do you suppose they think about us? That we're crazy and probably dead? Think about it, Race. Else Hann doesn't even wish she was here with you! That's your revenge." She fell back, laughing like a little girl.

Even Janinda smiled. "How about you?" Race asked clumsily. "Aren't you sorry you can't send your mean relatives a message?"

She shook her head, still smiling. "Like Jocela says, that's the cream of it. That they don't even realize they're being punished." And they thought of the ignorant, self-important, satisfied peasants of Ravenham with content.

It was the beginning of the happiest time of Race's life. Life in the mountains became a frolic, his powers ending the worst of the labor. The garden still had to be guarded, but it could be left for brief spells. With Joss and their mother taking turns, both were able to enjoy Race's power of flight as much as he did. Race found it more fun to fly with someone than alone. A long hunt now might take an hour, and fewer were needed; the problem of transport solved, he also had more time to dress out large animals he had rarely shot before.

He quickly learned that size was no bar to what he could lift or move, but it was more difficult to grasp the size and shape of large objects. Joss's exuberant suggestion that he move a mountain scared him, but it was not the old icy fear of the unknown, merely a normal fear of the consequences. Besides, he found it impossible to visualize a whole mountain at once, even when he had flown all around it and sensed its separate parts.

"Never mind, that will come in time," Janinda said.

Race didn't mind. The smallest object he could move was a little larger than the smallest he could see. Dust motes could only be nudged or bumped, not grasped; his mind could not sense such small objects. Splinters he could pull out easily.

Practice enabled him to fly with his mother and sister as easily as by himself, though he usually found it necessary to put an arm around each, thus binding them into a unit that could be moved as one body. Nor was it necessary to visualize their bodies in detail, to his relief; a simple image of a pair of cylinders tapering at the center was sufficient.

Stones and trees could also be moved by visualizing parts rather than the whole—knobs, the curve of the bottom, part of the trunk. But a mountain would crumble.

He quickly built up a loose, crude structure that was an improvement on the old shelter, though no bigger—they had only the tent for roof. He wanted to shave a rock into the kind of stone slabs that roofed the Ravenham houses, but couldn't.

Gripping a knob on one side and a projection on another, and visualizing them moving away from each other, would cause a rock to break up—once he mastered the technique, a difficult one. But the rock simply broke along its weakest lines into a number of jagged chunks. Often they crumbled to powder. He tried to visualize a plane surface through one stone, moving all on one side in one direction and all on the other side in the opposite direction; but it shattered along fracture lines at angles to the plane, with the usual result.

"There's some trick to it I haven't thought of," he said, and abandoned his experiments.

He quickly found it impossible to do anything with water or any other fluid; they had no shape he could visualize. Dirt was almost as bad. Small pockets of dirt lifted out on the shovel he could pick up, but they began to crumble unless they were held together by roots. Clods and grains would drop off,. and he learned to let them fall; trying to stop them scattered his concentration and caused him to lose the whole thing. Yet if too much fell off, the shape changed and again he lost it. Huge amounts of dirt, the size of the entire garden, could be lifted more successfully, if wet and clinging. The crumbling around the edges and bottom was proportionately negligible.

He could handle one object easily, two objects with only a slight effort, three objects with a distinct effort, and four with intense concentration. Five were beyond him, even if all were moved in the same direction at the same speed. But by doubling or even tripling objects—bringing them together and thinking of them as one—he could handle as many as twelve. Poor Nod got quite a hunted air.

Once Race caught up Joss and hurled her shrieking toward a distant mountainside at a speed so great it whipped tears from her eyes. Then, in a panic, he stopped her and brought her back at equal speed, unhurt. "Do it again!" she clapped her hands like a baby, but "No." She had been thrown toward trees and the mountain. From his angle, directly behind her, Race could not tell how close she was to either. She might have been hurled into them. His sensing ability was not accurate at any distance. He could not control anything he could not see or sense, and sensing was greatly inferior to sight.

Race's practice with his new talents took the form of play; when not flying or moving boulders, he was apt to be moving small rocks and pebbles about, chipping one another, or trying to throw them. It was odd that he had no sensation of effort in pressing them together. Only his eyes and ears could tell him how much pressure they were exerting on each other, and often a rock would crumble to powder against another before he could release the pressure.

It was difficult at first to move things quickly, even pebbles. At length he developed the trick of holding a pebble up and flicking it with his mind, as with a finger, causing it to shoot off like a bullet. Once he killed a deer with a pebble.

At Joss's suggestion he learned to kindle fires by pressing dry sticks heavily together, but in regard to wood he found his powers small. He still had to chop it with the axe, though he could transport it easily. Wielding the axe mentally was clumsy and slow, if not so tiresome. His attempts to break trees were not very successful. He would concentrate on a part of the trunk, forcing it sharply aside. But usually it broke in the wrong place.

Entire trees could be lifted easily out of the ground, though, roots and all. The roots held the soil together and moreover, they defined the limits of a volume of soil whose size and shape he could easily grasp. Race's attempts to pick up soil in large lots failed because he could not define the edges, nor could his sensing ability help him here. The garden, which he had picked up, had a different density from the surrounding soil; its edges were clear. No sign of any other powers were found.

"Some things are so easy I do 'em without thinking; others are so hard I can't do 'em at all," he said. "I could easily dig us a cellar or cave or something for the winter; I suppose I could steal food for us from the villages. We can get by easy, now. But my powers are no good to us if we leave the mountains."

Joss stared. "Why not?"

"Because I'm not a Starling and can't pretend to be

one. The first Starling I met would want to know where I came from and would probably holler for the elders."

"I don't see why!"

Janinda also was frowning slightly. Race scowled with effort. "Remember in our school reading books about the story of Arren Rosemont and the secretary?"

They nodded slowly, looking unhappy. The human secretary had given orders to other humans, supposedly on the authority of the Starling governor of Sonissa. The S. Rosemont had killed him for his presumption and there followed a goody-goody paragraph to the effect that men should not oppress men and that the Starlings wouldn't stand for it.

No one paid any attention to this protestation. The secretary might have been punished if he had given the orders on his own—more likely Arren Rosemont wouldn't have troubled his head about the government of humans. Few Starlings cared. There were many stories current, even in the Plantation, of the fates of men who attracted the notice of Starlings.

"Race is right," said Janinda slowly. "He might have full Starling powers, but he is still a human and the son of a human. We have no Starling blood for the last two hundred years. To them he'd be an outcast, or worse. What if all, or even most, humans began to develop Starling powers? Or the Starlings became afraid they would. You know what they do in the barns when an animal comes down with a serious disease."

They did. "Why, they might kill everybody in Ravenham to keep it from spreading!" said Joss, hushed.

"Yes. Whenever we go into civilization, Race will have to pretend to be human."

"That will take money. And I haven't found a single gram of gold."

Much of his practice had taken the form of flying up and down streams, face down, sensing the rocks, gravel beds, roots, sand bars, earth strata, and layers of bedrock, sometimes for many feet down. It had developed his sensing ability greatly, but that was all.

Janinda cleared her throat. "I think you just need more practice. We have stainless steel flatware here, aluminum and copper pots, iron and brass buckles and things, one silver coin, and Joss's gold ring. You should try sensing them every day, until you can tell the difference between them, and especially the gold."

Joss took off the tiny gold band that had been in the Sturtevant family four generations. Race looked at it with his mind. "It's pretty small. Doesn't tell me anything."

"Not on one glance, why should it?" Janinda returned from the shelter with the silver half-star. It too was a tiny coin, a mere five grams of metal. The stainless steel flatware was of better size, and the iron shovel was instantly perceived as metal. Working back down from there with various articles, he detected the metal nature of the flatware, and even of a bracelet, which he identified as non-iron, but not copper. It was brass, chrome-plated.

"That makes a good start," he said, cheered. For the next several days he carried the ring and coin about with him, looking at them frequently and comparing them with other small metal articles. And one day it paid off.

Bending over the stream where they usually washed in the mornings, he became aware of the presence of a pinch of sand under a flat stone six inches below the sandy bottom of the stream. For a moment he couldn't imagine why he should have noticed it; then with a thrill he realized it was vastly denser than the other sand.

Race swept the sand off the rock, making a hole in the bed, and lifted it carefully. The gold dust didn't stir, though sand spilled down on it. He couldn't pick it up by mind.

Lifting himself, Race whirled up to the camp so fast

the air whistled past him. "Where's a spoon? Quick! I need a spoon."

Snatching it from Janinda's startled grasp he whipped himself back to the stream as fast as he had come. Joss came running after, crying out to him in excitement. Race met her, cradling the spoon, which showed a thin streak of yellow under the brown dust in its bowl.

6

The first frost had already struck when the Wordens came down out of the mountains of Oroné. A rolling, pleasant land spread north of the mountains, patchy with woods, plowed fields, hilly areas, wasteland, large towns. Even the farming land was strange and patchy, with tiny fields of garden crops or grain, rather than the miles of level grassland to the south.

A smaller river here was organized like the main canal on the south, and it and its tributaries were served by the same Transport Company—at least its locomotives were the same scarlet and violet, a deplorable combination. Janinda nodded at this.

"The main canal joins a bigger river at the south end of the Plantation, and communicates by locks with a different stream at the head. Probably this river runs southeast too, and joins the same river the Plantation canal does."

"So Middleport would be somewhere downstream from here."

They decided to abandon Nod—Joss wept and was inconsolable—and Race carried the faithful bicaud back across the mountains and left him in the valley above Waterton. His brands would have been conspicuous north of the mountains. Joss came too, silent on Nod's back, more silent holding Race's hand on the way back. They were bundled up in blankets against the chill mountain air and Race flew slowly, musing on the wild slopes.

"I'm going to miss the mountains."

In the month he'd had, Race had found some fifty grams of gold—fifty to sixty silver stars' worth, over two hundred days' wages for an Equipment Op on the Plantation. With his father's carving kit Race made a little balance from a stick of wood, suspended by a hair from Janinda's head. As a standard weight they used the five-gram half-star piece, making the gold up into ten packets. Each was exchanged in a different village, half north and half south of the mountains, to minimize talk.

"If we'd had all summer we could've gotten five times as much!" said Joss.

"Or if I had been more patient."

"It's more than I'd dared hope for," said Janinda, smiling. It occurred to none of them that it was but one and three-quarter ounces. None of them had heard of ounces.

The land north the mountains was called the Vale of the Amaranth, the river being the Amaranth. In selling their gold they picked up quite a bit of information. The Vale was owned by the Riverine League and was more densely populated than the Plantation, yet large areas were waste. There were towns and cities, centers of manufacture, both unknown in the Plantation. The nearest good-sized town was Waterbury on the Amaranth.

Race flew them to it one night, staying low. They landed in a clump of trees on a high rocky hill. Their tools, the preserved skins of the summer's hunting, most of their cooking utensils and bedding, they had cached in a hole in the rock. They spent a chilly night.

Next morning they stared across the land, bemused at the way it rose and fell in hill and dale, the patches of woods and unplowed land. It was as unlike the smoothed and orderly Plantation as the mountains.

The locomotive road ran past the foot of the hill. They followed it toward Waterbury, avoiding the hustling engines. In the Vale, the canals hadn't been straightened. They knew that jumping rides was forbidden here; hay loads were rare and valuable goods were plentiful.

The Wordens were silent, daunted, in the town. Waterbury had all of five thousand people. Its streets were thronged with people, with draft animals, and once they actually saw an automobile, a small steam-powered machine that only a very rich human could afford. The people were dressed in many different ways, the women especially colorful. They strode along with rigid faces, not to stare.

A house loomed up on the edge of the canal road and they recognized an engine barn. Entering a door marked "Office" they found several windows marked "Tickets". One man stood behind them, yawning and sleepy-eyed.

"We wish passage for three to Middleport, please."

At that his eyes opened and they tensed, but he yawned and the spell was broken. "Can't do it. The through train has already left. Can sell you passage to Bridgetown on the local, though. From there you can make it to Middleport—cheaper, too."

"Very well. What is that?"

"Three stars. You've an hour before it leaves—time to buy food."

He pulled the cardboard tickets from a box marked, 1 s$, and wrote rapidly on each while they watched. Janinda took them, thanked him coolly, and led them out as naturally as she could. Race looked back and saw the man yawning again as he filled out his forms.

Joss heaved a sigh of relief. "Not a suspicion or even a question!"

"And two of those were Oroné coins, too," said Janinda.

Neither the Riverine League nor the Transcript Company maintained a mint, so money in the Vale was a mixture of vintages. Oroné coins with the head of Eldo Oro were not uncommon, and they had two Mavian Crown stars issued by the planet's Council. Race carried the money, which made him uncomfortable. Though officially a man, he looked too young to be the family head, so Janinda did the buying. Joss clung to his arm, more nervous than himself.

Food was sold in stores. The stores of the Plantation also sold imported food, mostly luxuries, so that was not too unusual. But some men brought in carts full of fruits and vegetables and hawked them in the streets.

"Prime melons, prime melons! Tenth-star melons! Prime melons, prime melons!"

They looked at the melons—medium sized, only seconds in the Plantation—and walked silently past.

"It seems that we have only a quarter as much money as we thought," said Janinda with restraint. "Even if they were primes."

"I couldn't eat 'em if I had 'em, at that price," Race said. Joss said, "Goddam!" But not loud enough for Janinda to hear.

Janinda led them into a small store and spoke pleasantly to the proprietor, an old man with a wizened face, at whose whiskers Race and Joss stared in fascination. "We're going to Bridgetown and we've never ridden the barges before. We were told to buy food—how much should we have and what kind?"

The old man's face lit up and he said, "You did right, you did right to come to an honest storekeeper. Those swindlers at the depot will charge double what their sickening food is worth. Let's see, let's see, Bridgetown is a long way, an all-day trip. So you'll want two full meals—and a little over to snack on. The great trick," he said, producing a straw basket and packing cheese, bread, sliced ham, apples, and tang leaves into it, "the great trick is to take enough for a meal after you get there, lest you be tempted to buy of those who sell about the terminal and be cheated. Best to eat just before docking. There you are, simple and sustaining food, but not without flavor for the most jaded appetite. You'll wish to pick your own condiments," waving at a row of tiny jars in all colors. Best of all, the basket totaled but seven tenth-stars.

The passenger barge was covered with a house that left but a small strip of deck on three sides; a front fence prevented passengers from climbing onto the forward barge to steal. Inside the house were two bathrooms and three sitting rooms; the roof could also be occupied. When they found that it was free, they settled there.

This trip was much like last spring's, except that the scenery was more varied and interesting and there were varied, interesting passengers. Out of shyness they held aloof.

Race studied his ticket in fascination. On one side was printed the name of the Transport Company—Arlen Transport, the first they knew that the Company *had* a name—the name of Waterbury, and the price, 1 s$ (one silver star). On the other side was a series of lines. At the top the agent had printed the name *Bridgetown*. Beneath that he had scribbled his name, and at the end he had struck it with a rubber stamp giving the date. At the bottom was a row of ten dots, the first two of which he had X'ed out. When they entered the barge, the first unmarked dot was punched out.

Whenever the barge stopped and they left it, another was punched on the return. A passenger explained that they could lay over and wait for the next train if they wished, but the ticket was no good the next day. There were eight stops, counting both Waterbury and Bridgetown.

Bridgetown was a considerable city, of some fifty thousand, on the big river into which both the Amaranth and Plantation Rivers flowed—Port River, it was called. All down the Amaranth they had noticed occasional powered ships pulling their own line of barges, painted a different color than the Arlen Transport Company's. Here at Bridgetown several water companies met, and there was also a line of locomotives pulling wagons into it from across country.

Race's head swam from the traffic, the noise, the swirling streams of humanity. The streets were full of draft animals, riding animals, electro-locomotives full of people, even automobiles.

Once, crossing the mountains of the Oroné to sell their gold, they had seen a gleaming point far away, crossing the sky. They had known it for a car of the Starlings who maintained their dwellings in the mountains. Now, they saw at least a dozen such cars slipping silently past overhead. Nobody on the ground so much as glanced up.

Looming over the square-topped buildings was a spire, just like in the schoolbook pictures; a slender needle of stone a thousand feet high and a hundred and fifty thick, wider at the top. Lights gleamed from windows there. There was no way up but by air.

When Race mustered courage to ask an indolent stranger about who lived there, he was rewarded with a stare and a laugh. "Nobody would live in a crummy hive like this! That's just the Offices. You know—the transport companies, Plantation affairs, banking, and so on."

Race stared at the silent stone, at the aloof demigods who came and went about their vast, mysterious affairs above the oblivious city. Who were they, what were they like? Could they be remotely like humans? He pictured stern, shining faces ... Joss squeezed his arm and he realized he was trembling.

They walked in silence for a space. After a long time Race began to become conscious again of the crowded, noisy, colorful city; its mingled odors, accents, costumes, vehicles, signs, building fronts. Women in tight scanty dresses lounged under shop-front awnings and stared amused at Race between his kinswomen; men hitched draft animals of a dozen types to metal posts and deposited copper half stars into them; children ran screaming after each other through the streets, under no one's control.

The silent white glare as the street lights came on almost sent him off again; Race had a vivid image of a Starling far above thinking a thought and all the lights flashing on into obedient glare. He glanced up and saw that the sky had darkened in contrast. The Spire was lit by upslanted lights around its base, but the top faded into the sky; only the glow of its windows was visible.

"Their ancestors were just like us," he murmured, awed.

"Don't keep stretching your neck," Joss murmured back, poking him in the side. "—Sir!"

"Don't rub it in—or your elbow either." Her feeble joke—"Sir!"—did help him. But it sent him off at a tangent. "Do people *really* bow to them? I wonder if they get mad easy. Do they have many human servants? How do they treat them? How do the servants act in front of them?"

Someday he'd have to know all that. *Face it—I've got to go there, sooner or later.* He was trembling again.

"Remember, in every way that counts except their powers, they are just like us," said Janinda quietly. "Your history books should have taught you about Starling wars and even some Starling criminals were mentioned, remember. They love and hate, marry and raise children, work and play, same as anyone."

True. But it didn't blot out those stern, shining faces of his fancy. Race came back to the present when a woman called to him—one of those wearing tight short skirts. "Don't let 'em lead you around like a *gent*, laddie," she said when she had his attention. "Come play with us!"

She was still laughing when they had passed. Race's face was hot.

Joss said, "You *must* be a rube—she spotted you at least half a block away. Your face is still red, too."

"Not my fault. I—"

Janinda said serenely, "You'll have to get used to it; you can expect such invitations as long as you look fairly prosperous."

"He doesn't have to look so pleased by 'em!"

She's more shocked than Mom. "Where'd you pick up your knowledge of the world, infant?"

Joss grinned. "Not in Ravenham—or Paulfields."

They were learning to overcome their shyness enough to ask questions of friendly-seeming strangers. One advised them to wait till an hour or so before midnight, then take passage upstream; the trip to Middleport was about eight hours, and that would see them there at about dawn, with the whole day before them. He warned them about sneak thieves on the passenger barge.

"I had forgotten that the barges run all night," said Janinda.

Even at that hour there were many people still on the city streets. Race slept uneasily, on the money; they rented a cubicle, barely large enough for the three of them. Janinda seemed rather taken aback at their having to sleep together, and still more shocked at the faint sounds that came through the thin panels of the barge. None of them slept much.

At Middleport they splashed water in their faces at the basin of a fountain, bemused by it—the first fountain they had seen. Then they were bemused again.

Middleport was a little larger than Bridgetown. It was beautiful. Here again they were in mountains, lower and softer-seeming than those of the Oroné. On three sides they sloped back around the city, which occupied a bowl, with a lake in the center where the Starlings had scooped out the rock in the river. It was not a big riverport, merely a wide spot on the Port River.

All around and in Middleport arose the Spires, slim and straight and tall against the relaxed mountains beyond. At least a dozen thousand-foot shafts loomed over the huddled houses of the human city. Twice as many, some as little as half the height, stood farther off, even on the lower slopes of the mountains beyond. The Wordens realized that Middleport was actually two cities, a compact human city around the lake in the river, and a tall delicate Starling city filling the bowl valley.

The Plates lay in a circle around the human city, farther up the slope of the bowl's sides, but were not really visible from this park beside the placid water of the river pool where the Wordens stopped. They had seen one close up, coming in, and could see the motion of Starling vehicles above them now. These were huge vehicles, bigger than barges, bigger than a barge-train.

The Plates were the space ports. Each was fifty feet high and from a hundred to five hundred feet wide; the sides were not vertical, but overhung, to prevent unauthorized human entry. That was also the purpose, freely admitted, of the spires. The Plates were made of glass or quartz, foamed in orbit—in free fall—while molten, until they were lighter than water. Such lightweight foam could only be blown where there was no gravity to pull the microscopic bubbles together. The light-weight stuff, in such slabs, did not stress the underlying rock the way solid stone would have done.

Road trains or canals ran by each Plate, and a huge electric hoist stood by each one. Space crewmen, men possessing a clearance fingerprint-checked by computer every trip, rode them up to the ships. Loading and offloading was by Starling, however, no stevedores being allowed atop the Plates. Streams of goods came down the hoists and were loaded aboard barges, or went up, to be stacked ready for loading.

The smallest spaceship could have carried several barge loads of goods; some as much as several barge trains. All were roughly the shape of a Starling car, swelling from a rounded bow to a circular midsection but with a flat bottom, tapering again toward the stern but blunt-ended there.

As they watched, one ship took off, tipping its bow upward in a smooth silent rush, curving and climbing above the bowl valley with less effort than any bird. It flushed pink on one side with the morning sun, shrank swiftly but silently, silently! Now Race began to understand the awe and admiration of his mother and sister at the sight of him in the air. It was all so smooth, effortless and powerful.

Joss made a soft sound of awe and wonder and delight. "I wonder where they're going, what they're taking there—who they are and what it's like!" There was joy in the lines of her body, pure joy that such things could be in the same world as herself.

Even Race began to share some of the thrill of a life where such things were possible. The terror of such power and the men who wielded it, power and the men he must confront, lessened. *Soon we'll be going out like that too! The stars! Soon!*

What'll we find out there? Surely only wonder and joy.

The early dawn was chill, with a hint of frost in the air, and this brought their eyes back to the ground. The human city of Middleport spread around them; tall colorful buildings with cupolas on top for Starlings to land under, the architecture, like that of Bridgetown, gothic and gay. Those big Starling trucks were occasionally glimpsed about the edges of the city, and two or three bright-colored, gleaming cars were in the air all the time. They saw small figures of bright-clad men or women—Starlings!—step out on a building roof, look down at the city, point, laugh, shiver in the breeze, and duck under a cupola over a shaft. And there were thousands of humans, dozens of automobiles, hundreds of draft animals, in sight.

"And they say Middleport is a small spaceport," said Janinda.

"Now what?" said Joss. They looked around, suddenly at a loss.

7

Jorden Macardel grunted as Race, hunching his shoulders against the shrill wind that blew up the Port River from the south, stepped onto the platform of the lift. He was a tough, gnarled, unapproachable sort, but Janinda had dealt with him. The hoist shot them rapidly into the air, causing some of the crewmen to mutter and stamp their feet. The smooth face of the Plate approached them; then the hoist slowed, stopped.

Below, the hoist slid along its rails and the platform crawled toward the top of the Plate, closing the unleapable gap. An attendant dropped a ring around a bollard, locking it in contact. They trooped off after Macardel's gangling figure.

Race looked about eagerly and fearfully. This was a small Plate, a hundred feet in diameter and holding only the smaller ships. Six or seven of these lay about the top, crowding it somewhat.

A Starling—he could only be a Starling—stood near the front end of one. One fist was on his hip and he looked, it might have been impatiently, toward the hoist. Aside from that he looked quite human, dressed much as they were but as well as any wealthy human. He was plump and his hair thin and gray; he wore a coat and his breath plumed on the chill air as much as theirs.

Then he was out of sight and Macardel strode unceremoniously up to the back end of another spaceship, opened it, and led them into its cavernous interior. Forward of this space was a bulkhead, through which he led them.

Before lay yet another bulkhead, a massive one with a door lacking any kind of latch. They stood on the flattened keel. There were four windows here, narrow, of thick polarized quartz, two on each side, high up and low down. Lines drawn between them would have made an X in the center of the compartment.

"C'mere, Worden," Macardel rumbled. "This is the cabin. Forrad is the bridge. Aft is the hold. Got it?"

Race nodded. Macardel bent and raised a long narrow trapdoor, the length of the cabin. "Keel batteries!" Opening another trap in the ceiling, he indicated a series of canisters. "Air makers!" To one side was a frame like a bicycle's, hitched to what could only be a generator. "Emergency generator!" Stepping to the door to the hold, he indicated the flattened sides of the ship and said, "Main generators!"

Along each side were the black copper tubes of the solar boilers. Race nodded; the system was obvious.

"See those fans?" Overhead again. "They've got to keep moving, keep the air moving, else we'll all suffocate in our own breath. The fans also carry the air to the purifiers there, and the purifiers need power too. See these dials, meters and gauges? They tell what every system is doing. They're your responsibility; if the air or power systems act up, we notify the Starling, try to fix it—and man the emergency while he gets us back into air. Got it? We have to keep him alive, but without distracting him. Look at those two red buttons." They were marked "Alarm". One said "Air", the other, "Power".

"They ring all through the ship. Mind you don't ring 'em without cause and jog his mind."

Race nodded. "Until I understand just what is an emergency, I had best ask you before ringing."

Macardel grunted.

Roop and Firolla and the crew chief seated themselves in chairs in the center of the cabin; there were six of these, fixed to the floor. After a few minutes they felt the vibration as a door forward was opened. Race, his excitement bringing on the familiar tension, sensed movement forward. The door in the bulkhead opened. He saw that it had a heavy bar with a polished brass knob for a latch.

The Starling stood in the doorway. He was an aging man, white-haired, thin, with a huge convex nose like a prow. The lines around his mouth had as much humor as sternness in them, and the look in his eye could have been kindliness.

He looked first at Race, who froze with icy belly, nodded in acknowledgement that a new hand had been added, fixed their positions in his mind, and nodded again to Macardel.

"Ready," the crew chief said gruffly. As the door closed and Race caught his breath, he felt a stab of admiration for Macardel. Most people's voices changed even when addressing human bosses.

He felt the latch slide home, the Starling receded, then the *Dinine* lifted smoothly, prow first.

"Don't try to leave your seat," Macardel warned him.

Race felt an unusual constraint, and from what he knew of Starling powers, surmised that he couldn't have moved had he wished. Air hissed past the hull, faintly audible, and he felt Mavia drop away with astonishing speed. The Starling was holding them fixed with relation to the ship, that they might feel no acceleration. Race had learned a little about acceleration, and had a vague idea that they'd be uncomfortable but for that. Actually, they'd have been pulped, as Firolla remarked.

Roop said, "I heard about a guy that was. He figured he could move when the Starling was concentrating on a lot of things—a big ship, a mind full—and he managed to wiggle out of his seat. *Scrunch!*, they say."

"What happens if there are too many people for the

Starling to hold them all?" Race asked, more than a little nervous but really interested.

"Sometimes they do it a different way that lets you move around, like in a starship, but that's kind of hard—I guess. Anyway, they mostly bring us in slow if it's a big ship."

Under them, running the full length of the ship between the banks of keel batteries, was a massive beam built up of bulks of timber pinned together. The whole ship depended from it. It was easily gripped mentally, though Race realized that at this acceleration the Starling must also be gripping the hull, a difficult shape.

The foot-thick hull was of quartz, foamed in orbit until it was lighter than water, reinforced with quartz or glass fiber and as strong as steel. But the ship's interior was of wood. Race had heard of radar and knew a little about radio, but it didn't occur to him that these materials were transparent to those wave-lengths. That was not wholly accidental, though a military ship would have had ceramic steam pipes rather than copper.

The windows in the curved hull began at knee height and went down to the deck, or started at head-height and went up to the ceiling, made of heavy polarized quartz. Race watched Mavia fall away, half in darkness and all soft, hazy and milky with cloud. He expected Macardel to growl at him, but the crew chief said nothing until the acceleration eased.

Race felt the constraint lifted, without being able to describe it—his limbs and head had not been so tightly gripped, but his body had shifted only with difficulty in his chair. Now he could squirm. "Turn on the fans," said Macardel, "start the pumps, the air purifiers—the batteries will take the load. As soon as the generators come up, turn on the gyros."

Race felt his way slowly around the board, again waiting for Macardel to take advantage and rage at his clumsiness or any error, but the crew chief waited in grim silence until his orders had been carried out.

"The ports don't pass heat or ultra-violet, and not much light, but don't look at the sun."

The cabin now was brilliantly illuminated from one side, shafts of light striking through the windows, glancing level across ceiling and floor. The boiler on that side was upping pressure rapidly, and Race soon kicked its turbine on, then the gyros.

Ten minutes without change; Race felt that they were traveling in the direction of the ceiling. He had expected a spaceship, like a car, to travel in the direction of its nose, as it did in gravity and air. But this way, they were held against the floor instead of the back wall of the cabin. While they were held in constraint, they had traveled in the direction of the bow.

Then the gyros snapped off—he felt the small heavy wheels up front brake to a stop—and the *Dinine* turned about. A vague shape moved across the ports, they steadied, and backed. *Clang* from aft.

Roop left his chair, propelled himself through the hold to the stern door. It opened on a port that gripped the ship firmly, preventing air loss. The Starling appeared suddenly—Race started—propelled himself without a motion through the ship, opened the port beyond the door, and was gone.

"Station," said Macardel matter-of-factly. "We'll probably take on special tools and goods for the factories."

They went back to the hold and found that a bored Starling had brought up a cargo net, full of boxes that just fit through the door. He was a thin, worried-looking sort, of indeterminate age. Macardel and Roop unhitched the net and began shoving the boxes into the *Dinine*.

The Starling didn't speak, nor did he seem to look directly at anyone, though he looked through Race once. When he had assured himself that the men could handle it, he took the net and himself back through the door into the station. This, like the bulkhead in the

ship, had no visible latch; on the other side was the
same heavy bar and knob.

That was all of the station that Race ever saw—a
large empty room with a couple of fluorescent lights behind grills. Race never figured out which was floor and
which was wall.

It was a laborious business, shoving boxes heavier
than themselves through a doorway they barely fit.
Race had all he could do to keep from doing it mentally, and asked Firolla why the Starlings hadn't done it
themselves. The crewman stared, plainly never having
thought of that.

"Why, they're Starlings! Whoever heard of Starlings
doing *work*? That's what they pay us for."

Race stared in turn. "Did you think those Spires
didn't take work? They work the same as anyone!"

"It's not the same—" began Firolla, but Macardel
interrupted, unusually.

"Worden is right, Starlings work same as anyone.
They could do this in half a shake. But it's tedious and
boring, and they've got more important things to do,
that they can't hire humans to do."

"Some of that must be pretty boring, too," Race ventured, and the crew chief grunted indifferently.

When all the boxes were in and strapped to the rings
projecting from the beam, and the timber frame that
lined the inside of the hull in the hold, they returned to
the cabin for another thirty minute wait. Presently the
Starling returned and cast them off, and they heard him
tugging here and there on ropes, checking the stowing.
He passed through without a word, nodded once to
Macardel, and latched the door behind him.

Race pondered, decided that Starlings were habitu-
ally silent before humans lest they be talked to death
by status-seekers. Even humans, as he had learned,
avoided conversation with their servants and employees.

They returned to earth, much more slowly this time
(they heard the boxes straining at the ropes). Race was

bemused to learn that this was a different and much larger city than Middleport, with at least a hundred Spires.

"Mays Post," Roop said—"First settlement." Mavia was named for May Rosemont.

The Starling unloaded when they had untied the boxes. Then he spoke. "You'll have time to eat." His voice was absent but pleasant.

Macardel and his crew joined another crew on the hoist, rode it down to the foot of the Plate, and stepped into a restaurant carved out of it, the walls like luminous milk. Race was surprised to find the prices reasonable, and they ate substantially if rapidly.

Race brooded over the unloading. It had fascinated him, but the Starling had done nothing he hadn't done often enough.

Then another hour's wait at the *Dinine* before the Starling again checked on them and took them out. The cardinal sin was to keep the Starling waiting; Macardel had a reputation to defend. This time they did not go to the station, but to a different place, possibly an orbital factory, half-visible forward of them. For an hour and a half they maintained power and ventilation while the ship hung motionless, returning without cargo. Presumably, the Starling had been working by mind from within the ship.

"And so it goes," said Firolla, yawning from boredom as they rode the hoist down in the chill air. It was not yet midafternoon.

Race burst into the room they had rented in a housing barrack. "Wow, what a day! Wait until you've tried orbiting!"

"Did you learn much?" Janinda asked quickly, looking up from the tiny sink.

"I learned all about spaceship function, and I picked up a trick about starship flight," said Race in a low tone. "We took a cargo to Mays Post!" He looked around the little room. The curtains they had rigged were pulled back, revealing two bedrolls and the bare brick walls.

"Where's Joss?" It wasn't wise for her to wander outside alone.

Janinda didn't answer for a moment. Then she turned to face him, for all the world like a child coming for a spanking. "She's at Macardel's."

Race stared. "She's working for them? I thought we decided she wasn't to risk getting a job. I'm making a star a day!"

Janinda moved to stand near him. Race started to stand up, but she pressed down on his shoulder. "Race, you know that there are five or more applicants for every opening next to the Starlings, especially in space work. Only some such man as Jorden Macardel could have gotten you there. And since he earns three stars a day, money means little to him. Those who need or want such jobs must buy their way in, you know that."

They had run low, though both he and Janinda had gone to work, Race on the riverfront, she as a street sweeper. She had recently lost her job.

"But—we had enough left to swing it. Didn't we? Macardel took me on, and he's really trying to teach me everything."

"No, Race, we didn't have the money. All we had was me—and Joss." Race sat dumb.

"The truth is, we sold her to Macardel. No point in mincing words." Her voice was as steady as ever but not serene; there was a grim effort to restrain grief; tremors shook it. Race, his head pressed against her, felt her quiver.

"Officially she's the Macardels' maid. Officially she's free to come home on Sundays. Actually—I doubt she'll want to come home, at first."

"But she won't be marriageable for a year!"

"Half a year. It varies with the individual; Joss could have been married months ago. I volunteered, Race, but she wouldn't hear of it. It's true she was worth much more. I thought long about it. She's your sister, but my daughter. And I trust you."

"What do you mean—me?"

She bent over him and her voice tauntened with an intensity of emotion she rarely showed. "You'll get us out of this pesthole of a city! You'll learn all the Starling tricks—soon—and take us away—somewhere—I don't know where, or how. I've done all I can for you, we've done all we can. It wasn't easy. Joss knows it—she depends on you. We know she won't be there long."

Race could see nothing but Joss in Macardel's hands. Macardel strong, silent, saturnine. *She'd die!*

"I'm going to go over there and tear his head off!" Race tried to stand up.

"*No*, Race! And throw everything away? The Starlings would be bound to hear of it."

That was true. Despite their seeming aloofness, they kept in close touch with the human society that spawned about their toes. They had heard ample tales in the past month to know that. Wealth among humans was tolerated; intelligence, ambition, even crime. But not anything that smacked of insubordination, much less outright revolt. Such a crime would be investigated. . . .

Race moaned in anguish, the tears squeezed from his eyes. "Joss," he whispered. "Oh, Joss. . . ."

When the first spasm was over, Janinda murmured, "It may not be so bad. Macardel is married to a woman younger than himself, who cares little for him. She married him for his social position and his money: a sharp-featured, sharp-voiced, sharp-minded little woman, possessive, jealous of her place. She'll contrive to foil Macardel of Joss as much as possible. She will be spiteful, but that will not be so bad for Joss. . . ."

It was cold comfort. Janinda led Race on to discuss his day, fiercely eager to know that he had learned how to use his powers. Haltingly, Race talked over all he had seen and done. It was a long afternoon. They went to bed early, morose.

In a month of practice in the mountains he had learned little that he had not known the second day after his discovery. It had become easier to generate the tension that accompanied the power, he had learned to concentrate well, but not well enough. Large boulders were his limit, nor could he shape stone, metal or wood, and star flight was a mystery to him. He could not build a spaceship even if he knew how to use his powers, nor could he navigate among the stars.

Most important of all, he had no idea of how to behave among Starlings. They had the knowledge he had to have.

They had concluded that there was no place for them on Mavia. There was no doubt in their minds that they'd be killed if the Starlings knew he had been a human. They could masquerade as normal humans, going to the mountains for gold, but aside from the cramping this life imposed on Race, it was too risky, the pattern of their life too odd. And now they knew that the Starlings kept track of strange or disruptive humans—who occasionally vanished.

It was not a reign of terror. The crewmen regarded the Starlings they met daily with vast respect, some awe, and no visible fear. That was there, but buried deep. It was revealed in silence, shifting eyes; humans rarely looked directly at a Starling, lest they attract his attention.

Middleport and the other cities had a corps of peacekeepers, polite men who wore large tin or brass stars on their chests, sweating in green and gold suits with gold "M"s worked into the sleeves. Far from brutal slave-drivers, transgressions brought them death. They heard no rumors of corruption, but many stories of humans killed for it. Troublemakers got equally short shrift, if more mysteriously. For any human who caused no trouble, though, Mavia might be called a paradise. Even freedom was not lacking.

But Race was no ordinary human. The only alternative was flight—among the stars. And they had come here so that he might learn the way.

For a time, lying miserable under the heavy quilts, Race remembered Ravenham. He found it more difficult than he had imagined. The Race Worden who had experienced life there was gone forever, and despite the pain within him, he would not return to it if he could.

Joss. . . . He clenched his fists. He would do it, learn everything he had to have from the Starlings, then there'd be a reckoning with Jorden Macardel. . . .

Next morning, Janinda carefully bathed his eyes with cold water and applied cosmetics to reduce the redness and swelling. When he stepped onto the platform of the hoist, Jorden Macardel greeted him.

He was in a dour good mood, might almost have smiled. "Good morning, Worden." That was unusual, and Roop and Firolla glanced from one to the other in wonder. Race nodded curtly in reply.

Not content, Macardel spoke again. "Chilly."

Race kept his voice even with an effort, staring at the milky glassfoam blurring past. "Wouldn't be so chilly if it weren't so windy."

Roop almost laughed. Macardel just grunted, but he looked at Race. Their mutual hatred was declared in that glance.

8

Race hurled himself into his study with a grim fury. For weeks he had gone without evoking that subtle tension that accompanied the power. It was not difficult to pose as an ordinary man. Even Starlings commonly walked, ate with forks, and the like, and he had found that the hands were more deft than the mind. To call up the tension and make use of the mind was equivalent to mounting and riding a bicycle, not done for trivial reasons.

Starlings commonly had two modes of action, physical and mental. It was said, and Race believed it, that a bullet fired at a Starling would simply rebound before it reached him. Once a bird had startled him by plunging out of a tree past his head and he had deflected it—like flinging up an arm in amazement, without the arm. With practice the Starling could deflect even so fast an object as a bullet, even when taken by surprise in "physical" mode, shifting to "mental" instantly.

Now Race maintained the tension most of his waking time, using his sensing ability constantly. Soon he found that the power lay just below his awareness, quivering on the string, and he felt he could match any Starling in speed of reactions.

Jorden Macardel dominated his life and his thoughts. The crew chief had made a bargain: spaceport clearance, a job for Race, teaching him about space, in return for Joss. With sardonic amusement he kept the bargain to the letter. Nor did he abuse his position to bully his subordinates, as Keithly on the Plantation had done. Yet the exercise of power was his only obvious pleasure. Race concluded that he would be fired when he had held the position a month and could claim "experience".

Theoretically Joss could quit, if he did. But real humans would not dare to antagonize a man who worked so close to the Starlings. They might be blacklisted. The same situation applied to Race.

Every evening Macardel politely bade him 'good night'. Every night Race lay awake for hours, raging.

The week followed the pattern of his first day. Once they made four trips in a working day of nearly ten hours; once the day lasted only four and a half hours. Once a young woman flew the ship. She was plump, scowling, richly dressed, and unbeautiful, with a prominent nose like the old man's. Sullen, she did not speak and they saw her but twice. Once the old man was accompanied by a small boy, about nine, who had not yet developed Starling powers. While they were transferring cargo and his kinsman was in the station, he hung about the *Dinine* and questioned them eagerly.

Jorden Macardel answered him briefly but fully. None of the others spoke to him except when directly addressed, rarely looking at the lad. He seemed aware of, yet unconscious of the difference between them, and might have been any boy, perhaps less diffident than most.

Sunday was the grimmest day of Race's life. He and Janinda sat in silence, the ghost of Joss all about them.

The second Monday, Race burned as he entered the *Dinine*. He found it difficult to keep properly subordinate, and Macardel's eyes gleamed with humor when he gave his orders.

This day the ship was again parked out in space while the Starling performed some unknown task. Race sat before the meters and gauges, bored and sullen. Macardel did not encourage idle chatter, and if he had, neither Roop nor Firolla would have spoken to Race lest they be caught between him and Macardel. Race scowled at his instruments, trying to sense what the Starling was doing. The vague motion of large masses came to him, nothing more.

There was nothing to do but listen to the occasional murmurs of Roop and Firolla, the hiss, thrum, whine of ship systems, occasional voices from the radio beside Macardel. He had studied the *Dinine* so often and so completely that he could almost have visualized it member by member. For the millionth time he sent his mind out, gripping the ship: so easy to send it forward by moving the beam—

Their heads jerked as *Dinine* leaped forward, then snapped to a stop. Race sat frozen in terror. For a moment nothing happened; Roop laughed. "Probably asleep up there and woke up with a jerk!"

Motion beyond the door. It opened and the Starling's mild, wondering face intruded. He looked questioningly at Macardel, Roop, Firolla, then around at Race, nearest to him at the bulkhead. His eye lit with wonder.

"Why, you must be a Starling! What are you—"

Race had been nervously fingering a glass bead he had found and intended for Joss. At the word *Starling* he performed the mental equivalent of flinging his hands forward, as if to ward off a blow.

Had he merely flicked the bead like a bullet it would undoubtedly have been stopped; but it bobbled in his grasp just before striking.

The Starling was hurled back against the door jamb, the bead making a soft heavy sound as it struck. He bent forward, floating weightless, as if ill. A bubble of blood welled out of his chest, swelling like a balloon; more blood oozed from his mouth and his eyes were distended. A few large and small drops of blood drifted toward the fans overhead.

Race made a choked sound of horror and brushed aside a distraction. A snarl made him look about into the contorted face of Jorden Macardel. The crew chief

had leaped upon him, raging, and had been brushed
unconsciously aside. Now, Race was holding him motionless.

Roop started to scream as Race struggled to adjust
his mind to the situation; then Firolla began to whimper. Race felt that his head would split; panic surged
through him.

The body had drifted into the cabin, clearing the
door. With a groan of relief Race kicked himself out of
his chair, grabbed the door, pushed himself into the
bridge. He floated motionless, back to the door and
eyes unfocused, panic images flooding his mind.

He pictured *them* surrounding him, glaring, the
corpse floating accusingly by. At any moment he expected a ship to pull alongside and Starlings to fly over,
to seize him. When a human attempted violence upon a
Starling, he was seized, tossed high in the air to fall to
his death; or he hurled head first at a wall, crushed,
splattered. Instantly! The Starlings rarely so much as
looked around.

A long moment passed and he was still alive. His
heart slowed. He had time to escape—the Starlings
didn't know what he had done. But the men would
tell—so soon as he was on the ground the hunt would
begin. Macardel would—

Race flung open the door and hurled Macardel away
from the radio. After one bound his heart slowed. He
pushed the three men into chairs and held them there.
Roop and Firolla made only the faintest whimpering
sounds, staring at him white-eyed. Macardel's visage
was grim and unreadable.

Race returned to the bridge, trying to think. His only
clear idea was that he must escape.

Before and below *Dinine* was the bulk of an orbital
factory. Behind and to the left lay Mavia. Behind and
to the right lay the sun. The Imperial Cluster lay off his
right hand. There was nothing before him and no one
seemed to be paying attention to the *Dinine*. A couple
of other ships floated by.

Race gripped the ship, extending his mind, holding the men in their chairs, even the corpse—it gave him no feeling of repugnance. To visualize it vaguely, which is what the mental grip was like, was not like touching. *Dinine* slid smoothly over the factory, picked up speed. Panic lashed him as his flight began; Race impelled the ship faster, faster!

Mavia fell away behind him with shocking speed, shrinking in his mind, at last becoming undetectable. The sun crawled farther aft. At last, minutes later and millions of miles away, he stopped, frightened.

He dared not return to Mavia for a time. He must return as soon as possible for Joss and Janinda. With those points settled, the question was: where to go in the meantime?

In Middleport they had found such institutions as newspapers and bookshops, and were surprised to learn that knowledge was freely available to humans. Janinda had bought as many books as they could afford. One had been a book of historical astronomy, giving the locations of many famous places.

Sonissa, from which Mavia was settled, was shown, and so was the section of sky in which Sonissa lay. It was a large, prosperous planet, with many Starlings. The picture distinctly showed fifty or more ships landing. He would be lost in that mob. Besides, it was the only place he knew.

Race looked about the bridge. It was comfortably furnished, rather like a lounge in a wealthy human house. A massive armchair dominated. The floor was covered with extremely fine soft fur, rich brown with unobtrusive markings in rust red. Two quarter-circular couches, in shaggy ivory fur, flanked the door in the bulkhead. The room was paneled in pale yellow and ivory wood, the floor covered the same in random widths and spacing; the whole seeming artless yet soothing. At first glance the room's wealth was not obvious, yet days before he had realized that the polished knob of the latch was solid gold. Doubtless the furs, even the wood, were of the same quality.

The flat ceiling and the flat floor jutted into the rounded cone of the nose. High up and low down on each curved wall were the long narrow windows, but between them was a round bull's-eye port on each side. Above the desk was another such pair of round ports; one about two feet across, the other eighteen inches, the small one above the other. These were teleperiscopes, Race discovered when he felt behind them. The hull was thicker here than aft, against radiation, and the optic systems operated around corners. The ports were very thick.

The big periscope gave the view forward, the small one viewed aft; the two on the side walls gave equally wide-angled views to the side. The long narrow ports gave a more restricted but undistorted view. Race looked around slowly.

The Imperial Cluster still lay off the right bow. The sun and Mavia were close together to the left behind. Sonissa lay in a configuration of stars to the right aft, passing by the sun. Quivering a little, Race started to turn the *Dinine*.

A light flashed but already he felt the alteration in the smooth movement of the gyros; they lay under the floor, beside the beam, and their motion made them as noticeable to his Starling sense as if they glowed. By the light was the gyro switch. He turned it off, but the gyros might take days to run down. Concentrating on them one at a time, he visualized them as massive little wheels, motionless; and they were.

The ship turned easily, Race breathing deeply to calm himself. Sonissa's sun was unmistakable, a medium-bright star just under a brilliant one. The periscope had cross hairs. Centering the star, he spun the gyros and turned on the switch.

Race sent his mind out over *Dinine*, visualizing it all, reducing the size of the image until the finer detail was lost but keeping the whole ship in his mind. It was the only way to travel fast without accelerating. He had done it once without thought, but now he did it consciously. Now he had an image of the ship, Mavia's star, Sonissa's in his mind, arranged in a triangle, with two points almost touching. He caused the detailed image of the ship to move toward the image of Sonissa's star.

When he had turned the ship, it brought Mavia's sun to the right bow, ahead of him; the Imperial Cluster was then on his left bow. Now the beams of light that slanted in through the narrow ports began to crawl across the ceiling and floor, away from the aft bulkhead. In ten seconds the sun was dead in the center of the right hand bull's-eye, in five more it had crawled aft of it. Race held the image of the whole ship in his mind and urged, hurled it forward, fists and jaws clenched.

Mavia's sun appeared on the small periscope, the view aft. It curved in from the right and down toward the center, shrinking rapidly to a star. Sonissa's star hadn't changed. Race expanded his image, causing the ship to become a microscopic point, yet stereoscopically clear—and to go faster, faster.

Mavia's sun shrank to a bright star, and to the side, distant stars began to crawl slowly backward. Some passed others, the closer ones moving the most. Looking ahead, Race felt a thrill of satisfaction to see that Sonissa's star was growing brighter, then very bright. Minutes crawled past like the stars. The brilliant star above Sonissa's brightened a little; they never passed it. Quite a dim star, however, did crawl past the left bull's-eye, a brilliant crimson coal.

Immediately after, Sonissa's star overflowed the pinhead aiming circle where the hairs crossed. Then it swung aside and they were sweeping past. Unconsciously Race had released the mental pressure; even so they'd have been through the system in moments. He stopped them and looked at the clock: the stellar crossing had taken about half an hour.

Race was exhilarated, shaky, exultant, fearful. He looked at the tiny spark of Mavia's sun. If only they could see him now! . . .

It took him more than half an hour to find Sonissa, however. He quartered the system looking for rapidly-moving stars, found a dead planet, airless, gaunt; then Sonissa, having gone most of the way around the sun. He approached it cautiously, expecting to be challenged, conscious of the corpse behind him. Should he blow the body out?

A light flashed, he jumped, and it flashed and flashed. It was in the radio section, but when he looked it was under *radar* and labeled *beac*. Radar, a kind of metal detector . . . *beacon*?

Race flung himself at the bulkhead door in a fury, tore Jorden Macardel away from the radio panel again, hurling him at the door to the hold. He struck it head first with a splintering, hollow *boom*! The door sagged open, split, splattered, torn from one hinge. Race shoved the crumpled body on through, followed it with the Starling's, more gently.

Roop and Firolla still sat in their chairs, whitefaced, strained. They expected nothing but death. Holding them there, Race returned to the bridge. He was shaking with fury and fear. After a long moment he decided to fly boldly in until challenged, then to streak for the surface. Once down it would be impossible to find him. . . .

The planet grew, a hazy, swirled marble. At one side was a vast white area like a great range of snow-topped mountains. Race edged the *Dinine* toward this wasteland. At a distance he saw a spark that might have been a space station. The radio muttered with voices, the radar beeped occasionally. But there was no challenge, no ship pulling alongside. Nothing.

The nose tried to move out of his grip and faintly, through the quartzfoam hull, Race heard air shrieking. He stopped dead, came down more slowly. Sonissa paid no attention to him.

Unbelieving, he landed by a stream and looked out upon a sunlit but stark land. Dark, gnarled trees, not pines, stood huddled under snow. A stream here was frozen, with snow on the ice. Yet it was level land. But the sky was of a deep pure blue that he had never seen, even at the highest he'd ever flown on Mavia. Race concluded that he was on a vast, high plateau.

"They'll never find me here!"

He thought for five minutes, nodded, then lifted *Dinine* and flew over a range of hills to a slash in the plateau where a stream tumbled down from it. It ran south, and he had seen signs of cultivation at the edges of the plateau.

Roop and Firolla shrank in their chairs when he looked at them, but Race had decided there was nothing he could say or do that would alleviate their fear or their subsequent hatred. Picking them up expressionlessly, he swept them out the hold door. Into the stream, contemptuously, he tossed the broken body of Jorden Macardel. It was promptly sucked under the ice.

"This is Sonissa. You'll find people downstream. It's a long way, but you should make it."

There was nothing more to say to them. Race withdrew, feeling a pang of pity. But it never occurred to him that they might not make it.

He returned to the first landing spot; then, cautiously, flew on lest the crewmen might remember it and lead the hunters to it. Far beyond, he came to a similar ice-roofed pool in a stream that also flowed south. Putting on his coat—a pitiful gesture—he flew to a large boulder and lifted it out of the ground.

As he brought the body of the Starling out of the ship, he detected gold in the pockets. It shocked him, but he needed money, and the thin chill wind didn't encourage hesitation. He slid out the money, considered the rings, decided that he had taken enough. He lowered the body into the hole, covered it roughly with evergreen branches, and replaced the rock. He didn't even know the Starling's name.

Shivering, he turned to *Dinine*. It must be hidden in such a way as not to be found, yet to be instantly ready for his use. Burial under boulders might take too long to uncover. Race concentrated on the ice sheet, lifted it as one. The water streamed. He moved *Dinine* onto the surface, where it floated like a cork, and lowered the ice until it touched. Thinking of them as one, he lowered them, forcing the ship under.

Then it happened. He had been afraid of the ice shattering, and now despite himself he visualized it happening. The ice promptly fell and broke up with a roar, spraying him with freezing water. Race shivered, but saw that the ship was hidden, great sheets of ice holding it under though it lifted them. A night's freeze and a good snow would hide it from all but the senses of Starlings.

Thinking the event over, Race realized his error. The ice was unbroken, and so long as he visualized it as whole, it would be unbreakable or virtually so. But when his vision departed from reality, the reality slipped out of his control. It did not break and fall. It fell and broke.

Turning his face downstream, Race lifted himself and arrowed away. The cold bit through him, tears whipped from his eyes. He slowed to about thirty but soon was shivering uncontrollably and had to land. He paced, pounding hands against his thighs, hugging his warmth to himself. For a time he wondered about Roop and Firolla. . . .

During that day he flew and tried to warm himself, growing progressively colder. At night, with no sign of the plateau's edge in sight, he was traveling down a rugged valley. For shelter, he lugged a boulder out of a hillside and crouched behind it. Here he built a tiny fire. Its smoke curled up into his eyes.

Sleep was impossible. He dozed, woke, dozed. His mind was full of somber images: the wondering but not unkindly face of the Starling just before his death, the pensive face of Joss as he had last seen it (how long had she known her doom?), Janinda's face, pinched and drawn, just yesterday.

How long would it be before he saw them again? He pictured them returning to the Plantation in defeat, and writhed.

Morning came in colder than ever, and windy. Pinched with hunger and numb with cold, Race flew downstream, often stopping to build fires. Mountainous clouds made up and presently snow veiled the world. He knew snow, but never had he seen so much; it was two feet deep already.

On the third day it was definitely warmer, and toward evening, exhausted by the cold and half-starved, he came upon signs of spring. The snow was thin, the stream open for long stretches, the buds large, and here and there an early leaf or flower braved the snow. He was out of the rugged lands, the stream flowing between gentle banks, but the sky was as hard a blue as ever: the edge of the plateau was still not in sight.

Shelter was more difficult to improvise and the night seemed as long and cold as the first two. The morning found him stiff.

A couple of hours later the snow became patchy, then ended. The land lay brown to the horizon, the evergreens were gone and in their place were lowland trees with tiny leaves. Yet still the sky was of the same chill, hard blue and the edge of the plateau nowhere in sight. *Is the whole continent a plateau?*

Ahead lay brown fields, fences, houses—smoke. Men.

9

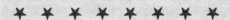

"—some unknown branch of the S. Chen family."

Race almost dropped the tray. It was so utterly unexpected. His knees almost failed him, the tea quivered under the covers over the cups. But the door had slid silently aside, he dare do nothing to attract attention.

The spasm was over in a half-second and none of the Starlings had glanced around. He advanced with a steady step. Norton Altamont was saying, "You know the Chens, Starling. Anything is possible of them."

"True. This one calls himself Hans Chen. But he didn't have the Chen trade mark blazoned on the doors of his car."

Race placed the tray on the table, swiftly and deftly transferred the cups of carmine tea and the tiny crystal vials of kip essences: turquoise, aquamarine, sapphire, cobalt.

The stranger was a slender medium-sized man, young, alert. His skin was olive-brown and his hair deep black, soft, wavy. His eyes were black and his features aristocratic and as regular as a painted doll's. He could be called beautiful. He was dressed in an unpretentious black silk suit, edged and slashed with silver.

"A young man," he was saying, "with a round face, small nose, but well-featured, with a deep underlying tan to the skin, golden-brown hair in a nondescript bowl cut. Brown eyes, taller than me and a touch heavier, probably pretty strong for his weight."

Race stepped back from the table, the gold-trimmed iridium tray under his arm. For the first time he looked directly at one of the Starlings: Lora Altamont. His mistress met his eye briefly, flicked a finger, and he turned and strode firmly out. He felt like running; he half expected to be seized in an intangible, unbreakable grip and dragged back.

". . . don't understand why you come to us, Mr. Slavin. . . ."

S. Slavin had been the only one of the Starlings to look at him. His glance was keen, penetrating, and prolonged. Race had felt he might faint. Yet he had made it through the ordeal without giving himself away.

He felt the door slide shut behind him and hesitated, thought of going back to listen. No; the door would open if he stepped on the nearest block—and the Starlings would sense him there. Rubber-kneed, he descended to the servants' hall, replaced the tray.

What do I do now? Run? Hide?

His impulse was to fling himself out the nearest window and fly away. But that would give him away, and they were looking for a Starling. Shakily he thought, *Stick it out. At least I can learn what they know.*

Since the S. Altamont family of Sonissa ran mostly to sons, they preferred human men to women as servants; it made for fewer "complications". Persistent rumor had it that this was highly agreeable to the older women of the family, but in his month's employ Race had not verified this. Still, the gray-haired Lora had promoted him here to Pearl Spire from the three-hundred-foot-tall Shamrock Shaft, which the family used only occasionally.

It had cost him fifty gold stars to buy that position, and it was the most menial in the house: blacking boots, replacing light tubes, etc. Nor was the Shaft very close to any Starling.

Ander Bode approached him. "Did you hear anything?"

Race tried to sound as eager and interested as the other servants. "He said he was looking for some renegade Starling named Hans Chen. I don't know why."

"A *Starling?* Do you know what Geremé Slavin is?"

"No, what?"

"Human Affairs Agent from Mavia—a goddam *shole!*"

An undercover agent among humans. Race pursed his lips, hoping his terror didn't show. "Wonder what he's doing chasing Starlings?"

Bode scowled. "Seems to me I've heard of the S. Chens before."

Race looked at him in surprise. In the two and a half months since the Wordens reached Middleport, he had done a vast amount of reading. On the other hand, most humans bothered to learn only enough to do their jobs and were surprisingly ignorant and credulous.

"The S. Chens were a great clan a long time ago—before the Rosemonts. They led the wave up to the edge of the Imperial Cluster—they started the terraformation of most of the planets around here—Sonissa and Mavia both. But now they're just a kind of Starling rabble, half respectable, untrustworthy, a bunch of double-crossers."

Margaritta, the plump aging cook who was a fixture in the S. Altamont family and virtually an Altamont herself, looked over Race's shoulder to say, "Mr. Norton calls them *lokees.*"

"What does that mean?"

"He says that Lokee was a mischievous, untrustworthy god in an old pagan religion. He's very well educated, is Mr. Norton." This with pride.

A bell chimed discreetly and Bode hurried away. Race spent an anxious half hour until Margaritta assigned him to help with serving lunch. This was set up in the Great Morning Room, with its huge window giving a view of Sonissa: above, a deep blue sky, the ground fifteen hundred feet below like a rich ancient rug, grass-green with forest-green markings. All was blurred and hazed by distance as if by time.

The little salon where he had served tea was just off this room, and when Lora Altamont came in to supervise she left the door open. Race didn't drop anything, nor did he give other evidence of this tension, but he was in as bad a condition as he had been when he first served a Starling: Linetta Altamont and a male friend, at the Shamrock.

"Put Mr. Slavin's chair here, Race," said Lora Altamont. Her voice was quiet, but so were the rooms. "It carried well and reverberated in Race's head. In a daze he carried out her instructions and at last escaped.

Race! And S. Slavin couldn't have missed hearing that. Insane of him to use his real name here. He was registered on Mavia as a crewman of *Dinine*. Why else would Geremé Slavin be here? If he asked a question or two of his employers. . . .

Race frankly shook for an hour, desperately fighting down the idea of flight. Presently it was known to the servants that the mysterious S. Chen had broken into a bank and gotten away with a hundred gold stars. They were quite indignant, it being a human bank.

Slavin left after lunch, but the talk continued as the servants put together scraps of overhead conversation. Norton Altamont had a low opinion of Slavin, not because he debased himself by posing as a mere human, but because he betrayed humans. "A dirty business." Confident of his Starling powers, he could afford to be kind. Many Starlings loved to exercise their superiority viciously, as Race had heard. "But creatures like this Chen must be put down."

His duties left him plenty of time to brood. Servant gossip told Race that Geremé Slavin had a picture of Hans Chen, drawn from shopkeepers' descriptions, that Chen had killed another Starling on Mavia and stolen a ship. He learned that the crewmen of the ship had been turned out to die in the far north, but that a band of fur-trappers had saved them.

Race had presumed them dead for a month and felt guilty. Now he felt no relief, and in fact wished them comfortably dead again.

Finding himself on Sonissa, Race had concluded that he could best learn about Starlings and the details of landing a spaceship and taking off, by getting a job as a servant to Starlings. He also wanted to find some place to which he could take his mother and sister. He already knew it would be possible to pass them off as servants; now he knew they could be called members of his household, children of his kinsmen.

Having broken into a bank by night, he had bribed the Marjordomo of the Shamrock Shaft into hiring him. A bad choice, as days might pass without a Starling in the place. It was a low spire with an elevator to ground level. But pure luck brought him to Pearl Spire and into much information, a lot of it from the servants, many of whom had been with the S. Altamonts for years.

Often he had dropped out of his window at night, posing as a Starling among humans. He had ordered a human firm to build him a typical Starling car—for three hundred silver stars—and flew around the spaceports, landing here and there to watch the big interstellar passenger liners land. As a Starling he could not eavesdrop, so reverting to human form, he asked questions of the pompous human employees.

To his amazement, there was virtually no red tape. Ships were rarely tracked or challenged on approaching a planet, though it might be different in time of war. Nor need ships land at the ports. Most Starlings owned private ships and government was weak among them. The individuals were too powerful to be coerced.

In addition to these sources of knowledge, there were books. Race was surprised, on entering bookshops catering to Starlings, to see many of the titles sold to humans. Knowledge was not kept from humans, but few were interested in such things as astrogation. Race bought a couple of books giving the main intersteller trade routes in the region on this side of the Cluster, plus an elementary text explaining how to cut across previously unknown territory. He made little of this, never having studied geometry, but studied doggedly. Books on history and exploration he read to find some ideal planet to settle on, without coming to any conclusion, and he studied science in general, partly out of interest in how the universe worked.

Novels, written by and for Starlings were also circulated among humans, and gave him as much of his information as any other source. He was recurrently amazed to find them quite human.

As usual, that night, word was passed among the servants that any who wished would be dropped to the city below. They would be picked up in the morning. Race applied this time, an unusual event. Half an hour later, one of the S. Altamont boys in his late teens slid a car off the Spire and dropped them into Rhodia. He laughed and chattered with a bent old manservant visiting his brothers.

They piled out at a plaza, arousing no interest in the passers-by, and caught trolleys in various directions. Race rode out to a depressed area, the nearest thing to a slum on Sonissa, to a room he rented in a small house. The old woman who kept it was unclean, but cheerful and gratifyingly uncurious. Here he kept his books. He dropped them into a cloth bag and paid off the old woman, then took the trolley to the end of the line.

For a time he had debated about going to the garage where he kept his car, but when he realized the danger, he was dizzy with fear at his error. Geremé Slavin had said, "The doors of his car," and he had that picture from shopkeepers' descriptions. Starlings kept their cars at home, where they'd be convenient. He'd been very conspicuous, in a small way. Doubtless that car was under watch at this moment.

" . . . don't understand why you came to us," Norton Altamont had said, and Race hadn't heard the answer. Now he realized the meaning. Slavin was circulating among Starlings with his knowledge, trying to make him panic and run.

Race hesitated and considered returning. If he was looking for a Starling . . . But Slavin knew that he had posed as a human on Mavia. It wasn't worth the risk . . . besides, he could return to Mavia and Joss and Janinda before anyone expected him. . . . His fingerprints were on file—Slavin must have copies. That decided him.

Pity I can't use the car.

Outside the city limits he lifted a big rock out from among tree roots, picked up the rest of the gold—the bank robbery had not been his only crime; he had a pound of coins left—and waited for full darkness.

By morning he was far to the north, into what he had once thought a plateau. What had taken him thirty-six hours before took but twelve, now that the weather was warmer. But it wasn't necessary to go all the way.

Race was flying up the stream into which he had sunk *Dinine*. It seemed higher than it had then, but he paid no attention to the logs and litter along the banks until he felt *Dinine* on the bottom of a quiet pool. Shocked, he landed, lifted it. The ship was whole, but the doors were stove in; it was full of water, and the generators were wrecked.

For over an hour Race tried to repair it, cursing himself for not having realized the ice would melt. But even after he knew the truth he had persisted in thinking of the planet's winter cap as a high plateau that summer never touched. Useless! Many feet of boiler tubing were stripped away, the gyros were out of their bearings, the batteries in God knew what shape, the internal paneling warped and split, the wiring shorted, the radio full of rust. The air renewal system could not be used—

No. I'll have to think of something else.

The first thing was to get off Sonissa fast. He had money enough to buy passage, and humans who could afford it were allowed to do so. *Where to? Mavia?* Reluctantly he decided no.

On reflection, he considered Neolan. Race had been surprised to learn that a passenger line ran there, but the old rancor was long gone. Neolan was a doublet system under the old Rosemont Crown, and a busy and prosperous one. Easy to lose himself there.

He was wan and nervous when he approached Rhodia that night, but had no trouble. The hundred and more slender, translucent spires towered indifferently overhead. They were not made of plebeian stone cut from mountains, but of super-fiber-reinforced silica or alumina, formed in space: hideously expensive but incredibly strong and beautiful. Creamy or pearly they were, translucent, some in elusive pastel colors difficult to focus on, changing hues as the cloud shadows swept over them.

Bright-colored dots sped over, some showing as oval; some rose from or dropped to the roofs of buildings in the human city: there were shops with domes or roofs having cupolas that covered shafts. Starlings needed no elevators.

On a low Plate lay a huge liner, some five hundred feet long. It was flown by several Starlings in turn. Starlings who did not care to fly their own ships settled toward its upper curve. Goods and other cargo were taken in below: Race was part of it.

He was the only human passenger, and from the beginning it was evident that the crewmen resented him. Oddly, there were no special human quarters. He was given the least desirable suite in the ship: the most luxurious quarters he'd ever had, and only his familiarity with the S. Altamonts' opulence kept him from staring at it. For a spaceship it was amazingly spacious.

Race stretched out on the silk coverlet and mused, his tired brain seething with images: the Plantation, the Mountains of the Oroné, the Vale of the Amaranth,

Middleport, *Dinine,* Rhodia. Now, Neolan. How long before he saw Mavia, Joss and Janinda, again?

He awoke, roughly shaken.

"Wake up, rich man! Up!"

Race flung out an arm but was hustled to his feet. "What's going on?"

The crewmen laughed. "Off, rich man, it's going off! This is Jacarantha, and off the ship you go!"

10

✳ ✳ ✳ ✳ ✳ ✳ ✳ ✳

The port prison had been built by Starlings. Its walls were two feet thick. The stone blocks—four or five feet high and ten feet long—were covered with the fine parallel lines typical of unsmoothed Starling work. The blocks were cut, Race had learned, by taking a fine, heat-resistant wire in mind and forcing it into the stone, slicing it like cheese. When friction had melted the wire, the Starling lost it and slid another down into the groove. The traces of rust had long since come off the blocks; the prison was old, older than the houses of the Plantation on Mavia, and sweated with a clammy musk of fear and pain.

Race paced around it, incongruous in his finery. He had been noticed just once, when a jailer had offered to buy his clothes. Fear tore at him; he kept resisting the urge to butt down the wall and make a break for the port.

Voices, the sound of footfalls, a heavy tramping and rough shouts, laughter, the clangor of iron bars.

"Company for you, Yale," said the jailer who had braced him about his clothes.

"Yo? Wot's he like?"

"Oh, the bird of fire!"

The company of prisoners halted at the cell door and two were allowed to enter. "That's my bunk yer on, dullhead!" said one instantly, a coarse blond no taller than Race but half again as broad across the shoulders.

"Firebird is right," said the other sourly, taking in Race's clothes. "Wot are ya, a shull?"

107

Race gaped at him, having arisen. "Are you crazy?"

"If yer a shull for *them* yer as good as dead," said the blond. His was the voice of Yale.

"Oh. I thought—on Sonissa a shole is a Starling, incog."

"Yer from Sonissa? Shoulda stayed there, wean. Why'd you come to Jackoff, fa crysake?"

"I didn't," he said bitterly. "I was bound for Neolan but got thrown off ship to make room for more of *them*." They began to nod, smiling sourly. Race managed a bitter, humorless smile. "Naturally I was arrested for lack of passport. They fined me everything I had left. Tell me, is there any way I can get off this dung heap?"

They shook their heads in counterpoint, something like pity showing in their gazes. "Not unless you got friends among *them* t' come askin' questions."

Yale sat down, eyes fixed intently on Race. "You got rich on Sonissa? It's really that kind of planet? And you just walked up to the port and bought a ticket t' Neolan? God," he said, a bleak gray look coming into his eyes, his voice a taut whisper. "There's nothin' I wouldn't do to set foot on a planet like that. That's all I'd ask. Just to *be* there. I'd take care o' myself after that, and never complain about the work they give me. God, God!"

Race had never felt such pity in his life for weak and defenseless creatures as for these tough, self-assured men. He remembered a comment on Sonissa about Jacarantha: "The S. Jacksons keep them under pretty tight control . . . not a bad idea, I sometimes think. Oh, of course they don't mistreat them! Production falls when humans are mistreated, everyone knows that. . . ."

"What happens to me now?"

They looked at him speculatively. "They'll put you to work. Better git rid of them feathers. After yer registered, yer contract'ull be sold. Most ever'body gits sent to the mines. Well, if it's a strip mine, it won't be too bad."

"Ya got a trade? Wot k'n you do?"

"I've had space experience. I was going to Neolan to study; specialists get more."

They had instantly begun to shake their heads. "Not on Jackoff you don't, not space work. That's all taped up. And even if you was listed 'reliable', you'd never crack the space gangs; they don't spread the gravy around."

"Wot else can you do?"

"Nothing . . . wait a minute, I can handle a steam tractor."

Yale pursed his lips dubiously. "I dunno much about the plantations . . . but I reckon anythin's better than underground minin'. Them poor bastards never see daylight but once or twice a year."

They were interrupted by the arrival of food: two portions of heavy soup and half a loaf of coarse bread. Rations would not be issued to Race until he was registered. The prisoners shared as a matter of course. Conversation shifted to their work. It developed that they had been confined as a mild punishment for recalcitrance, laziness, troublemaking, or the like, in their original work gangs. Though they worked at the port, this implied no privileges; they were stevedores who never got near any ship.

Yale was serving a three-year sentence; he casually remarked that half his working life—beginning at age ten—had been spent in mild or hard confinement. "In punishment", they called it.

Immediately afterward the lights flickered and the men rolled into their bunks. Race climbed into one of the two upper ones just as the light went out.

He lay there long, staring into the gray darkness. Again, harder, he had to fight back the impulse to break out and flee. He expected at any moment the door would clang and Geremé Slavin step in and point coldly at him. But Slavin wouldn't know he was on

Jacarantha until the ship reached Neolan. He mustn't panic. He'd done enough damage by panicking. He must stop and think things through carefully.

First, what had happened on Mavia when the *Dinine* hadn't come back?

No doubt the owners got in touch with traffic control and reported it overdue. No doubt they had checked around in space, in case the Starling had had an attack. Not finding him, it was marked down as a mystery and forgotten. There was simply no lead in any direction.

Until Roop and Firolla had told their stories on Sonissa.

Race sighed. Even now he couldn't muster any anger against them; they had been so terrified. . . . Well, that story had been reported to Mavia forthwith and Sonissa authorities also began to check. Fortunately, his use of the name Hans Chen had thrown them off. No doubt much of their time was spent in investigating the raffish S. Chens. Even now they would not have thought that he might have been a human, or born of humans.

But the human expert, Geremé Slavin, came to Sonissa. He was probably merely their best investigator.

Then I panicked and ran again. Would he have been safer if he had stayed on Sonissa? He couldn't decide. He felt strongly that he would not. Certainly he would not, if he had not been warned that they were closing on him. It was amazing how calmly he had gone about his business, as if there were no communication between the planets!

Was Slavin after him now? It gave him a thrill of alarm to realize that the Starling was. The S. Altamonts would not take many hours to realize that Race Worden was their Race Worden . . . *why* had he been so insane as to use his own name!

Biting that back, he concentrated. He had left the Pearl Spire at night, flew north all night, flew south all the following day back to Rhodia. At the time he was buying his passage he had not yet been missed; shouldn't have been missed until the second morning he wasn't at the Spire. Unless one of the S. Altamonts asked for him especially the first day. That was unlikely, but say it happened. (He felt it safer to consider the worst.) If so, and if his absence jarred their minds into realizing that he was the one they wanted, they'd have gotten in touch with Slavin immediately. Even acting on a suspicion.

Slavin would have taken time to trace his movements about the city . . . no, he had already laid his trap—the spaceport must have been put on alert before Slavin started making the rounds of the Spires. Chills went down Race's back at his danger then. Fortunately, Sonissa's human officials hadn't been very alert. Probably they hadn't been told Race was a Starling. Even so, it had been so close that he could only lie and shake for some time.

It was worse than that. Slavin had set an orbital trap, must have, and had been waiting for *Dinine* to travel unsuspectingly out to them. If it hadn't been ruined. . . .

Okay. With the spaceport and Chen's car and other haunts watched, and his orbital trap ready, Slavin must have thought he had the situation under control. It might be some time before he learned that Race had escaped, bound for Neolan. *No.* The computer which handled passenger traffic must have notified him immediately that one human had left. He would instantly set off for Neolan. It would take the ship a day or so to get there; he'd have to wait for it. Having learned that Race wasn't aboard, it would take him several more hours to return to Jacarantha.

Race added it up and it came to noon tomorrow—at the earliest.

Again he almost panicked. It was easy to believe that Slavin could have had good luck and be at arriving any time. Of course it would take time to get action from the local officials. What should his plans be?

They were hampered by lack of knowledge. Tomorrow he'd be registered; that involved signing a work contract, which would then be bought from the planetary corporation by one of the S. Jacksons. He'd be transferred to their company, most likely mining. After which, he must disappear. Fake an accident, say. . . .

Wouldn't fool the S. Slavin, but it'd keep'em from putting me under watch until he gets here. He hoped there'd be time for all this.

And if there's not? He thought of Yale. *By God, that's it!* Yale knew his way around the planet. Race needed a ship . . . Yale had worked for a couple of years about the port—and would give anything, even loyalty, to be free—he'd need a crew. Yale knew people it'd be safe to approach. As soon as he was registered, no, Yale would be taken out to work at the same time. Well, the first thing in the morning—

Hell, why wait?

Race contained his eagerness and thought carefully. *Yes.* Speed might not be essential, but then it might. Neither did he want his fingerprints on file, they had been recorded on Mavia when he was cleared for space work. His clothes were those of a Starling, and he doubted that Starlings on Jacarantha had to be registered.

He landed on the floor light as a cat and shook the blond man's shoulder. Snores were instantly choked off and two powerful, hairy paws closed on his throat. He stopped them unconsciously inches away and whispered fiercely, *"Yale! Yale!"*

Yale's voice trembled with fury, almost inaudibly low. "A goddam stinkling. One of *them!*"

"You want out of here, man?" Still whispering.

"And inta worse trouble? Beat it, ya crawlin'—" He sat up by pulling on his captive wrists, put his craggy face within inches of Race's. It was barely visible in the dimness. Bitterly he whispered, "Goddam it, isn't it enough I'm in for three, but ya gotta git me in worse?" Plaintively, "What are you bastards made of, anyway?"

Race admired the other: no cringing. But he hadn't had time to think. "I'm not a provock. Hell, man, I'm in worse trouble than you. I need your help! Serve me faithfully and I'll take you to a planet where humans aren't even registered."

Long pause. Then, suspiciously, "What kind of help could *I* give a *Starling*?" There was a touch of awe in his tone, especially on the last word.

Impatiently Race said, "Come, you know Starlings have wars, crime, rebels, and general hell-raisers, same as people; only we're not kept under such control. I never expected to be here; I need someone who knows his way around and to crew a ship for me. We'll have to steal it. You with me?"

"It sounds reasonable. I dunno. But if it's a trick to git a bunch of us sent to the mines. . . ."

Race had been thinking fast. "Okay, look, you don't need to do anything but follow me till we're outside. Then, at least, you're free. You can follow me or not."

"Just bein' out when I'm supposed to be in 'ud git me sent to the mines. Man—Sir—you don't know the Jacks if you think bein' out's bein' free. Here a man—human—can't buy, sell, work, travel, anythin', without his fingerprints. Even walkin' down the street, if a flack waves you over to a checkpoint, they can haul you in."

"God! Well, how about this? Say I drag you out? You know, if I was a provocateur, I could get you in deep without any trouble. My word would be enough."

"Yo, that's true." Pause. "Okay, I'm with you. Now what?"

"Say what you'll do for me," said Race, reverting to Plantation modes.

"I'll follow you wherever you go, help you, do whatever you say that I can. I'll give you the best advice I can. I'll help you steal a ship and make up a crew, and fly it wherever you say. Now what'll you do for me?"

"I'll take you to a planet where humans aren't registered and give you a fair chance to be free. You understand, if you kick up trouble about the Starlings they'll cut you down fast. But anything else, even crime among humans, they don't worry much about. And there's plenty of work. If you agree, let's have your hand.'"

Yale put it forth hesitantly and Race gripped it with an unexpected surge of warmth. He had not realized how lonely he was.

"I never saw a Starling close up. You're just like a man—Sir."

"Just call me Eagle." He had given the name Eagle Krane on boarding the ship. "And back before there were any Starlings, all our ancestors were alike."

"I never knew that, Sir—Eagle, Sir. Now what do we do?"

"How about this fellow? Be rough on him if we disappear, but can we trust him with us?"

"Ropy?" The other prisoner still snored. "Yo, I guess he can be trusted. He's a good worker with somebody to watch him. He's not so crazy to git free as me, but he's got a fam'ly he ain't seen in years. He'll come—and he'll not betray us, or I'll break his neck."

Yale awakened Ropy and converted him to Race-worship quickly. "You goin' to bust down the walls?" Ropy asked, awed.

"Why not holler, 'come and get us'?" Race said. "How does this door open?"

"That's no good," said Ropy. "It's got a iron bar up out of reach—not a lock you can pick."

"There's a handle fastened to it—you push up that and the bar turns, then you slide it."

Race had already detected the bar. "Which way does it slide?" It was all a jumble, through the heavy iron top plate of the barred door.

"Left. Left from outside, Sir. Eagle, Sir."

Race rotated it slowly, almost half a turn. He could not tell when the catch no longer engaged, and was afraid to push the bar hard, for fear of tearing the staple out of the stone with an ear-cracking screech. Presently it slid slowly. They all heard the door click. It sagged open, hinges groaning faintly.

They stepped through and closed it, breathing rapidly and feeling oddly unsafe outside the cell. Snores resounded through the dark around them.

"How about these fellows?"

Yale reflected. "Most of'm are all right. But you can't take'em all, and none of'm—none of us—has space experience. You promised to bring Ropy's fam'ly, you know, Sir. Uh, I've got a family, too, that I ain't seen in a year. I know it ain't in our agreement, but if you would—"

"Sure, sure. Should've mentioned it." They were walking quickly and silently down the corridor, Race probing the darkness before and behind him for the hint of light or movement, with human and Starling senses.

"Thank you, Sir. Thank you. We'll likely need a fair size ship, Sir. The rest of our men'll have families, too."

At the end of the corridor was a guardroom converted to an office, closed and locked now. No guards were in evidence. As Yale had said, being out was not being free; it was a ticket to the mines. No doubt there were guards somewhere about—asleep, most likely. Beyond the offices where their work was tallied was an arched opening Race remembered. Beyond lay a courtyard surrounded by the building, a series of arches opening into corridors like this one, lined with cells. At two places on opposite sides, the building fell back to the streets and the outside gates fronting on them. Through these the trucks came to haul them to work.

"There'll be guards at the outside gates," Ropy said. "Sir."

"Tough on them."

The Imperial Cluster was just above the roof to their left; just above it was a small but very bright satellite. They poured cold silver radiance into the gray courtyard, striking pastel flames from Race's silken "feathers" and turning the baggy prison blues of the others to misty gray. Race took their arms, hefted their bodies in his mind, then lifted them lightly into the air.

They gasped and Yale became rigid at the feeling of external control. Then they were above the tiled roofs, and they gasped again at the sensation of movement without effort. Race halted them. "Any likelihood of our being seen?"

"I wouldn't think so . . . Sir."

"The first thing is to be able to get off this stinking planet. We'd better steal the ship first. If we fail, I can't keep my promises to you, but at least I won't have gotten your families in trouble."

"Good thinking. What size ship do you want, Sir?"

"The smallest, the easiest to hide. Two crewmen can handle the smallest ship I saw, but not many are that small. We may need half a dozen of them. But there'll be plenty of room for the families."

"Well, we don't know any space men. Ner we wouldn't trust'em if we did."

"No matter, that's easy to learn."

Race drifted toward the nearest Plate.

"Sir," said Ropy, "maybe you should fly higher. They can see us from here, but higher up we're just three—uh, a Starling and a couple of servants."

"Not likely anybody'd report us, now we're away from the prison." But he lifted them so rapidly the warm air whistled by their ears. From their new altitude they could see the ships on the Plate—two huge freighters in the 300-meter class and a couple of medium-sized bulk cargo ships.

"No good."

Farther away was another Plate, lit up: a liner was preparing to leave. Still farther away was another Plate, dark. A car went by overhead, a distant oval. They cringed but nothing happened. Presently, they were near the Plate.

"That one do, Sir?"

To his disappointment there was none as small as *Dinine*. The one Yale indicated was a yacht half again

Dinine's size, but Race shook his head. "That's some-body's pride and joy. It'll be missed in the worst way, and watched for. On the far side—that stubby-looking job. A small, fast freighter with maybe a couple of suites for Starlings—and it has an old look. Now, is the Plate guarded against Starlings?"

There was no way to tell. Shrugging, Race plunged them boldly down beside the freighter. It was about thirty meters long by eight in diameter, and its boxy hull was almost square in cross-section. Race was re-lieved to find that it was not locked to Starlings. The typical Starling latch was a lever or wheel to be manipulated from outside of the door; an absolute bar to humans.

Race opened it, saying, "That's a good sign—they're not alert to the possibility of Starling crime." Sniffing the musty air that came out of the ship, he almost yelped with joy. "The ship's been mothballed! Great! They may not miss it for days."

His crewmen entered warily, sniffing the stale air. They were in the crew area; overhead was the flight of-fice, aft, the crew's quarters. Farthest aft were the holds, and farthest forward were the Starling quarters and bridge.

In the flight office Race nodded with pleasure. The batteries were flat—the ship had lain here for months and had not been left on trickle charge. The steam pressure was nil, of course, but the boilers showed a full volume of water. He was afraid they might have been drained—distilling hundreds of gallons of water is a lengthy chore. The instrument board was locked shut, but the keys were at hand. A flashlight lay beside them and the weak light through the ports was supplemented by its pale beam.

Race examined the radio, radar, and transponder. The latter had been left on, as had the former. He turned off the transponder and the radio transmitter. Going forward—followed timidly by his crew, who were still more fearful of being alone in the dim ship—he checked that the main board showed them off.

"Everything's covered with sheets," Ropy murmured to Yale.

"Yo, and the beds're bare."

Race made sure that all the light switches were off. Back in the flight offices he showed them the emergency generators. There were four of these, each with its bicycle frame. "But you won't need to crank them. I can do it easier myself, for a short time," he told them. Taking hold of the armature of one with his mind, he started it spinning, faster and faster, until its voltmeter touched the green. Then he fixed on his mind the image of it turning at that speed. Already the batteries were beginning to show a faint charge.

"It would help to stir the air, though, if you'd take turns cranking one. One's all I can handle." Not strictly true, but he didn't want to tire himself.

For nearly an hour they cranked away, growing more and more jittery in the pale light. At last Race decided they had enough charge. Concentration on the generator was almost unconscious, leaving his mind free to consider their next move. He decided that he didn't care to take off like a normal spaceship; he didn't know Jacarantha's drill for traffic control. No one would pay attention to a ship in atmosphere, he thought, and so it proved. With transponder off but running lights on, it was just another truck or barge.

11

Jacarantha's sky was yellow. Race stared at it, bemused. Near the eastern horizon, where the sun was just rising, it was a deep gold. Overhead it was yellowgreen, almost olive; elsewhere, yellow with the brownish cast of topaz. Race felt a wave of homesickness for the natural skies of Mavia.

They were about forty miles from the city. Here was an abandoned mine known to Yale. Race had widened one of its upper galleries and moved the ship into it, and they slept as well as they could for the rock overhead. Their battery charge was low again when Race awakened and he was still generating.

He still felt sleepy, and kept shaking his head. He had gone thirty-six hours without sleep before shipping out from Sonissa, had caught only a couple of hours of sleep on the ship. Last night's ten hours' sleep still left him minus.

"Now, back to the city," he said. Down in the ship, at his extreme range, he visualized the armature as brick-shaped and instantly lost control of it.

"You've got nothing to fear while you're with me. Only trouble is, Starlings don't go flying about with servants except in cars. We can't take a chance on stealing a car. Is there any place where we could find a hull—discarded or not completed?"

They thought about it and Ropy hesitantly mentioned a factory that built personnel transports—"flyin' wagons"—used for shifting prisoners or work teams quickly. "Nobody pays any attention to them, Sir."

Race was enthusiastic. "Great! No ordinary Starling would fly around in something like that, except when working, so no one'll think anything of one being gone."

They made good time back to the city, flying low; in less than an hour they were circling to come in toward the factory. At high altitude Ropy pointed it out to him. Race parked them in a tree top while he flew boldly in.

Naturally, there were no Starlings at the factory. Race landed on the roof beside a cupola, dropped down the shaft and found himself in a plush reception room. The receptionist squeaked and stabbed at a button excitedly. Though their wagons were turned over to Starlings regularly, they were not used to seeing them around.

"Yes, Sir, yes, Sir. What may we do for you, Sir?" A well-dressed man came hurriedly into the room, bobbing and bowing, nervously rubbing his hands. "Come to look the f-factory over, Sir, or—"

"Jonathon Jackson," Race said in clipped, businesslike tones—not threatening but immensely self-assured. "Do you have the wagon ready?"

"Sir? We have wagons—"

"Good. Where is it? I need it immediately—mine cave-in. Hurry!"

The manager trotted ahead of him down a carpeted hall to a balcony up in a hangar dome, at the end of the building. Here two personnel transports sat waiting, and a third was just being pushed into the room on a dolly. It and one of the others were blazoned with trade marks. Race flew instantly down to the third, and moments later was out of the dome. He shut the door behind him and lifted the transport into the sky, to streak halfway across the city.

The plebeian vehicle, drab in steel-blue and steel-gray, seemed to attract no attention.

This city of the S. Jackson humans was composed mostly of long low barracks, up to five stories tall, made of dingy black-red brick or gray stone. It was well shaded, but the dusty, dark green trees were equally dispirited. There was a vaguely shabby, dingy air to the city, though neither streets nor buildings seemed particularly worn or run down. The gray streets were scrupulously clean.

It was partly the effect of seeing blue-clad people, their dull shapeless garments lacking touches of color; partly their demeanor, lacking the gaiety he had known on Mavia and Sonissa. They even walked dully. Partly, too, it was the occasional appearance of a couple of black-clad "flacks", the sight of the whipping post's long shadow in an unfrequented square. Not that there were many police in sight—but they were never out of mind.

There were several touches of color about the scene—the white barracks, or apartment houses, of the wealthy humans, the bright gleams from several stores that probably catered to Starlings, metallic flashes from the radar antennas of the old fort, and the flow of color from Starling cars and space ships. The four spires that reared above the city were cut from stone, as were the cheaper shafts of Mavia.

There were many ships coming and going about the city. The S. Jacksons had a planetary factory here, and exported a wide range of manufactured goods, including precision instruments. Though the mines bulked large in the minds of the human populace, they were comparatively unimportant to the S. Jacksons.

Race recrossed the city to land by the tree in which he had left his crewmen. They dropped from it and ran toward him.

When they had caught their breath he said, "Now, where are your families?"

Ropy's family lived on the outskirts of town. Race landed before the barrack and flew arrogantly in, Yale and Ropy lying down to hide in the aisle.

"The wife and family of Ropert Pervukhin," he said sharply to the housing official. Word of the escape had already reached him.

"Y-yes, Sir."

Ropy's wife was a drab, thin little woman with a sharp nose and many fine lines around her eyes. They were dark, hollow, and anxious. Her cheekbones showed and her shoulders were round. They sagged still further when she saw his finery and her anxious expression deepened. She was not half as old as she looked. Three small children followed her, the two smallest wearing nothing but short shirts, all equally shock-headed.

"I don't know nothin', honest Sir I don't!" she began to whine fearfully, pushing her children behind her futilely.

That pathetic gesture enraged him. Race's frown deepened. "Come along," he said brusquely.

"But Sir, please Sir—"

Impatiently, he caught her up and slid her gasping and whispering toward the wagon. She stared at it wide-eyed, the children running silently but desperately after, clutching at her sleazy skirt. She stopped short and moaned in fear on seeing the men in the aisle. Race snatched the wagon into the air so fast she staggered, but if Yale had not grimly held Ropy's head down he'd have jumped up before all the spectators. Despite their distance, they'd have known something was up.

The woman shrieked and fell into his arms. While they were babbling, Race gestured Yale toward him. "Thanks for keeping that fool's head down. Now, where's your wife?"

"Outta town—she's a cook fer my old road-makin' gang." He indicated the direction.

The site was a "village" consisting of four dingy brick barracks and a couple of company stores. An electric locomotive pulling a line of huge rubber-wheeled wagons rolled toward it; two such roadways crossed here. One was being widened and another track laid. Steam tractors pulling personnel transports were drawn up before one barrack; the others were occupied by plantation workers.

Race landed before the road-workers' barracks, having instructed Yale and Ropy to stay down. Ropy's wife sat with her children huddled about her, looking appropriately dazed and apprehensive.

Silence greeted Race—it would—but something in their attitude told him that here again word of the escape had preceded him. The workers fell away, leaving him confronting a nervous foreman who kept bobbing his head and trying uneasily to smile.

"The wife of Hal Yale, quickly."

"This way, Sir. I'll take you to the building Super, Sir. He hasn't been here, Sir, indeed Sir. We'd have held him for you, Sir—but—"

With relief he turned to the building superintendant. "The wife of the prisoner is being summoned, Sir," said that worthy—Race had seen the word travel ahead of him. "If you'll p-please to wait here in my office, Sir—ah," with faint-sounding but immense relief. Race's expression had been kept under taut control in a manner most frightening. The servility and fear they exhibited caused him to frown and shoot stern short glances at them. They quaked in his wake.

Mrs. Yale was a young, surprisingly attractive woman with tawny-blonde hair, a queenly figure, and a manner almost composed. "Yes, Sir? You wish to learn about Mr. Yale?" A tinge of pride in the way she said "Mr.", and the officials blanched.

"No," said Race bluntly. "You come with me."

Her face didn't change appreciably; she nodded in a way that showed she had expected this—and still was glad her husband had tried escape. Her piquant defiance reminded him of Jocela daring him. Race checked and ostentatiously consulted a piece of paper.

"The boy too."

The officials glanced at each other and his estimation

of them went up a hundred and fifty notches. The woman turned with dignity and called; a boy of about two years ran in breathlessly. He had been held back in the corridor, and clearly the officials would have kept him from the mines if they could. But Race saw no hatred, only resignation, in their faces as he led the way out. Mrs. Yale carried the boy, his face pressed to her neck. Her head was high and her stride firm.

He got them in the air quickly, but Yale had ducked down behind a seat. Their greeting was short and almost unemotional, as if they had met yesterday. Yale made a few hasty explanations and came to Race's control seat. This was in a cab of sorts at the bow, with a door that could be closed; it and the bulkhead were of glass.

"So far so good," Race said, before the other could thank him. "But the rest will be harder. Even a Starling can't just walk up and demand a person without a reason—he'd have to show a requisition, or even that the contract had been bought. Right?"

Yale thought it over and agreed cautiously. He knew little about how the planet was governed. "Anyway," he said, "we need men who're edicated, to handle the ship. Me'n Ropy don't know nothin' about nothing. Ner we don't know many edicated men. Wait a minute—Ally comes of a purty good family—she used to talk about men that had been places and learned things. Ally!"

She came forward cautiously, glancing warily at Race, whose expression had relaxed. When the problem was explained she frowned in concentration and thought for a long time. Finally she said, hesitantly, "The only educated man I can think of is that one that came from Neolan—you remember hearing about him—to teach *them* in their schools. I remember thinking, the poor man. They arrested him for something, fined him and made him take a normal contract instead of the fancy one they hired him on. Jo-something, he was."

"I'd have to have his name, or have him pointed out."

They couldn't remember his name. "It was four years ago."

"Where would he be?"

"At the school—the Starling school. Over beyond the fort."

"Okay. I think I can get him out. But we better wait until night—he may be busy now."

They had been flying low and slowly, as if inspecting the fields. Race now circled the city and landed in a ravine in a rough section, hoping it wasn't a Starling park. But the S. Jacksons had a whole small continent to themselves.

"With this crowd, we'd soon run down the batteries in the ship. I don't want to keep coming and going around the mine; somebody might notice."

"Somebody might notice us here, too, Sir, but not Starlings."

"Humans here?"

"Yes, Sir. Runaways, deserters they call'em. Every now and then *they* get mad about'em and get up a big hunt to chase'em down, but it don't stop'em. I think the humans in the hunt act like they don't see nothin', and the runaways just join the hunters."

"Even here people find ways to be free. I should think you'd have run away long ago."

"It don't solve nothin', Sir. Soon's my kids was registered, they'd be sent straight to the mines with me. Kids don't last long in the mines."

Race examined the forest carefully but saw no one. *Means nothing; of course they wouldn't let themselves be seen.* "Well," he mused, "we don't care if they see us; they aren't going to report us to *them*."

"Well—I hope not, Sir."

"How could they?"

"Through the black market. They got friends, steal them tractor fuel to cook on—no smoke, see?—and food, and clothes, and like that. They might get a message to someone."

He must have been on the steal himself. "We'll have to chance it." Race looked around again. "If they show, maybe we can talk some food out of them. Pity we don't have any money."

They composed themselves to wait out the day, a very long and hungry one. Race set small bushes on the flying wagon, spread limbs over it, and caught up on his sleep. The others talked about names of people who could man a ship and survive freedom. The list was short, and they did not know where any of them were.

"We haven't got long to spend huntin' them up before they miss our ship and realize wot's goin' on," Yale said.

The pressure of time rode them all, as they began to realize the enormity of their acts. Race slept poorly.

Long before dark, Race took off for the Starling school, alone, feeling his breath coming fast and his heart beating. But he was reassured by the sight of the school. Though it was a palatial and beautiful building, it was built low. No Starling would spend the night in such a building, certainly not on this planet. It lay in beautiful grounds within a high, outward-leaning wall that was not obvious from within—the school was on a hilltop and the wall was around the bottom.

Beyond it lay the shadow of the old wartime fort around which the city was built. It was not a particularly massive structure—nothing could withstand Starling powers—primarily a port and barracks for Starling warriors, a place where they could rest. Slender towers held horizon-scanning radar under domes, all long since mothballed. Planetary defense must be conducted from orbit.

Landing before a low, plebeian but not dingy building, Race alighted and summoned a doddering ancient from his task of trimming the hedges. "I'm from Neolan," he said, "and I'm looking for a professor who comes from there. He's been here for four years. Jo-something." He made feint of checking through his pockets.

"Joquirl, Sir?"

"Something like that."

"Why, he's over in yon apartment house, Sir; number twenty-seven. Many's the time, Sir—"

Race flew toward the building, carrying the wagon behind him, before the attendant could lead him over there and spill too much. Faces were visible at windows, not close up but standing back in the rooms. Here and there a neatly-clad individual lifted a hand in startled fashion, not knowing whether to come up and offer to help, or to avoid him.

Giving them no time to decide, he stepped straight up and opened the door of unit twenty-seven. Each unit had its own outside door and consisted of from two to five rooms—very classy accommodations for Jacarantha. But Starling youth must be insulated from the grubby reality of the world.

The two-room unit was occupied by a silvery-haired man, slender and small, with an apologetic manner and a small white beard. He sat reading, in a shabby robe, and looked up in mild wonder at the intrusion. "Yes, Sir? May I help you?" Standing up, he saw the Starling vehicle outside the window and became effusively polite, bowing with practiced grace.

"You're the one from Neolan? Four years ago? Joquirl, isn't it?"

"Yes, Sir, Joquirl Wun, Sir, at your service, Sir."

"Good. Pack your things and let's go."

"Sir? You've—come to take me away?" He caught his breath and his voice broke. "Thank you, Sir. Oh, thank you, Sir!" Tears leaked out of his eyes. Looking closely, Race saw that he was not so old as he seemed.

Joquirl was so overcome that he could scarcely move, but he doddered around, with tears and words of gratitude, picking things up and putting them down. Race said, "I haven't much time. Here." Snatching a sheet off the bed in the inner room, he started emptying dresser drawers onto it. When everything was in it, he rolled it up and fastened it with belts. Coming through the little front room he saw a shelf full of books which he scooped up, shelf and all. Other books lay here and there on the table and the floor; he piled them up on top.

"Er—those aren't mine, Sir; they belong to the Institute."

One was a volume on astrogation; another on reference astronomy. He had to have them; the ship's references had been removed. "You've earned them," he said gruffly, and took them along.

Joquirl called out a farewell to a couple of his neighbors, asked to be remembered to someone, waved tearful goodbyes, and climbed into the wagon. Race lifted off quickly and flew toward the city before curving around to the ravine.

"What's this? Aren't we going to the port?"

"No." Race glanced at him. "The fact is, I'm what you'd call a renegade Starling. *They* are after me. I'm assembling a crew, and I'll make you the same promise I made the rest: serve me and I'll take you to a planet where humans aren't registered and give you a fresh start."

Joquirl gasped in horror at being in the clutches of a monster. It took him some time to start thinking again. Despite its oppressiveness, Jacarantha had provided a comfortable routine.

"What—what are you going to do with us, Sir?" he quavered.

"I need men to handle a spaceship—that's all."

"But I don't know anything about spaceships!"

"You do know astrogation, don't you?"

"Er—yes. I taught it—but—"

Race performed a half-circle that took them behind a hill, dropped and whipped them into the ravine. Sunlight slanted heavily in from the horizon, a creamy golden mist over all the world, obscuring objects at a short distance. The very air seemed to have curdled.

Yale met them eagerly. "You got him? Good! Does he know any other good men?"

"Good men?" quaveringly. Joquirl shrank from the features of this wild man.

"Good men with space experience—men who'd come with us and glad of the chance!"

"Why, why no. I am—I was a teacher at the Institute—the only space men I knew of were those who were sentenced to The Cup for insubordination two weeks ago—none of the other teachers ever—"

"Cup?"

Yale slapped his leg. "You've hit on it, Sir! They'll come and glad of it! Why, they won't even be missed—likely."

"What is the Cup?"

"Er—a method of execution by ordeal—by exposure. Starvation, usually."

"It's a dungeon on top of a shaft—they drop'em in there and feed'em when they remember—and when they go on vacation or just forget—" he shrugged expressively.

Race felt his temperature rise—rage against the S. Jacksons was the usual emotion on this damned planet. "How can we get them out?"

Silence. Then Joquirl cleared his throat. "Ahem. They are fed at irregular hours. No one would be surprised at any time to see a Starling car hover over The Cup or even descend into it to, er, discharge food."

"It wouldn't stay there long, though," said Yale. "The stink's pretty strong."

Race pondered, nodding slowly. All this time he had had the fearful feeling of that inhuman hunter, Geremé Slavin, circling around him, waiting, waiting, toying with him. But even the Starling had his limits. It was quite likely that he had no idea that Race had acquired a ship—Race grunted. The moment he knew for sure

that Race had been on Jacarantha—when he learned of
the prison escape—Slavin must have had every ship
checked. That must have been around noon—say
morning to be on the safe side.

No! He trembled and his knees were weak at the
narrowness of his escape. Slavin wouldn't have gone to
Neolan and back to Jacarantha. He'd have followed the
liner, lest he jump ship. *He must have gotten here by
midnight at the earliest!*

Would he think Race was still here? He'd had a couple of hours to escape. No—there was plenty of evidence that he was still here. Or was there? For instance,
the wives of the escaped prisoners had probably not
been questioned by a Starling, but by human officials.
Until Slavin showed up and fingered Race, no Starling
paid attention to him, escaped or not.

Had their wives' disappearances been reported to the
Starlings? Why should they be? The human officials
merely marked their contracts, *arrested for interroga-
tion by Starlings.* Had Slavin checked up personally?
Why should he? And he was busy with other things.

How about Joquirl? He came in contact with Starlings every working day—but he wouldn't be missed
till tomorrow. Or say his disappearance was reported by
Institute officials—they had an explanation. Though
the S. Jacksons might be annoyed with Neolan, they'd
surely see no connection with Race. Slavin couldn't
foresee *everything.* The last, defensively.

"Okay, I'll go pick them up. Yale, you come along
in the back, as if you were being delivered there, or
ready to throw food out, or something."

"Names and offenses of victims are posted," Joquirl
said. "He should act like he's ready to feed them."

Taking no chances, Race moved the entire party farther from the city and in a different direction. But no
one seemed to notice when the stolen steel-blue and
steel-gray personnel transport flew through the city
again.

The Cup was of black stone, with walls ten feet high. Its inside diameter was thirty feet. It was set on a fifty-foot shaft of the same stone, some ten feet in diameter. This shaft was set in a dark, stagnant pool from which evil fumes arose.

When they looked into The Cup, they saw that there were three slits in its floor in the shape of a Y—for sanitation and drainage of rain water—and the disposal of bodies. Often men were squeezed through them still half-alive—or fully alive, to conserve food. The bodies were fished out of the pool and disposed of.

When they had been first left here they were by turns sullen, glum, and depressed. They spent much time pacing about the sun-heated stone or peering wistfully down through the slits, hoping to see relatives, friends, or anything besides the dull stone around them. They quarreled often and fought bitterly over trifles, such as a share of the shade or a word; quarreled and fought to keep from their minds the knowledge that this was their whole world and their future: it had narrowed to this tiny Cup shared with six other men.

They were brought here to die. Some days were required for this to sink in, for them to realize that it was really true. The glimpses they caught of the world through their slits were all the living they would ever do again. For the rest of the time there was the stone-walled Cup, the sun or the rain, chill night or gasping day, and each other. The quarrels tapered off, ceased.

They began to spend hours just sitting, staring at nothing. Much of the time they thought about food. Now the pinch of all the meals they'd missed in The Cup began to tell. What had been an annoyance that set their tempers on edge now began to occupy all their thoughts. It was not alone hunger, but the uncertainty that any food would be brought to them again.

They thought less and less of loved ones at home, guilty about the lapse at first, then less so, then not at all. Finally they were unconscious of the lapse, and at this point they were little better than wild beasts.

They sat or lay in their places, the weak ones in the constant sun, the strong ones in occasional shade. Each watched the others, lest the little stale water that collected in the center be drunk up. They no longer fought over the infrequent food; they no longer dared not to share: someone would have died. And their strength declined. Thus they lay when a shadow came over The Cup.

The stench around The Cup was more sickening than that from the pool below. Even Yale gagged as they dropped into it. Race was as reluctant as Yale to leave the security of the wagon in this place of horror, but he flung open a door and leaped out, seizing men and pushing them through the air into it.

The horrible thing was that they continued to lie there, spaced as far apart as possible, not even lifting their heads of hope they had none. Race even thought they seemed fearful of leaving The Cup for other, unknown, horrors—here they had come to terms with their fate. Yale worked as grimly as he, wasting no time on exhortations.

He flung in several bundles of rags—no body was expelled till it had been stripped, and rags had accumulated over the years—and leaped in after them. "Lie down and stay down," he rasped, and staggered forward as Race lifted the wagon upward.

"They won't be missed till next time they're fed— and that won't be before morning," Race said over his shoulder.

"They look pretty thirsty—it rained yesterday, o'course, but not for a week before that."

Of course—the only water vessel was the hollow in the center of The Cup. Race put them down by a stream some distance from the city, searching to find a place far from any plantation villages. "Everybody out and into the water," he told them, and he and Yale began pushing them out. They stood uncertainly on the mossy bank, looked at the slow, sun-warmed flow of yellow water, at the sun bisected by the purple horizon, at them. Were they to be drowned here?

"Get clean," Yale said, throwing the rags into the water and herding them in. Clothes and all they ventured, drinking, rubbing themselves tentatively and *slowly,* with many glances at Race and Yale.

"Okay, you'll do." Yale dragged one out by the hand. "Where's yer family, man?"

"Family?"

12

It was after midnight before the families of the seven crewmen—those who had them and wanted to take them along—were rescued and safely in the ship. There were over thirty people, including grown and married children, but there was room for all. Despite his daytime nap, Race was tired and very hungry. He had had no food since the evening before, some thirty hours. But it was now or never. He wanted to leave by night, before his activities were traced. He also had no way of getting food without alerting the Starlings.

He put Yale in charge in the crew's quarters and brought Joquirl Wun to the bridge with him, locking the bulkhead between. "This is going to be tricky," he had told Yale. "Don't frighten the rest, but *they* 'ull be watching for us. This ship is invisible to radar though—it was built for smuggling." It still had firing ports forward. "But they can get us with clidar near the planet. It's going to be chancy. If anybody wants to back out. . . ."

None had. He must avoid the port. Coming out alone from some unfrequented limb of the globe would have given them away at once. Race flew low toward the city, climbed over it, then switched on his running lights well above it, hopefully lost in the stream of traffic. First correction to his visualization: there was no *stream* of traffic. He saw and sensed three or four ships as many more might be out of his range.

They were running right into Slavin's trap. His stom-

134

ach lighter and more hollow with fear, he extended his mind, enfolding the fast little freighter within it, moving it as he had moved *Dinine* between stars. No acceleration was felt within the ship; instead, they felt Jacarantha's grip weakening, draining away. Race crowded the safety limit, the air-speed indicator whining.

The transponder beeped in warning before they were out of atmosphere and Race felt a wave of despair. It was off, not replying to that insistent question from space. But where radar probed, coherent light beams also would be. The yellow sky had long since turned green, then blue; now, royal purple set with stars.

The transponder carilloned and the radio barked at him harshly on the official space frequency: "Attention freighter, halt at once or—"

Another voice cut in as authoritatively, but Race wasn't listening. From low, fast orbit overhead a ship had flashed up behind him; he felt it swell. A fast-moving dot before him would be another. He was keyed up intolerably and turned the ship now without a thought.

At his right hand was a handle in the hull. Moving it swivelled a teleperiscope that combined a low-powered wide-angle view with a high-powered narrow-angle one. Immediately below their line of sight and precisely parallel to it was a glass tube about an inch in diameter and five inches long. Connected to it was a pocket in the hull, containing a handful of common glass marbles. The whole apparatus was outside the airseal.

It was the work of but a moment to line the telescope and tube on the growing dot of light that was the first ship. He had placed marbles at the bases of the firing ports before takeoff, and now he flicked one as he had flicked pebbles like bullets in the Mountains of the Oroné months before, but with the fury of despair.

Involuntarily he blinked—in time to save his vision. The Starling ship erupted in a fireball that illuminated half the world below. For half a second Race stared horrified at the destruction he had wrought. Then fear blossomed like that spreading glare: every Starling in the area knew where he was now. He swerved the ship away recklessly, not hearing the clangor of the radiation alarm.

His mind swooped and reeled as things like planets whipped past in less than an eyeblink—two of them, almost on opposite sides of the ship, one nearer than the other. On the radio two voices were bellowing, one, "Surrender!", the other, "Shoot! Shoot!"

Another *thing* flicked past, invisible, indetectable but to his mind—seeming to have planetary mass yet to be incredibly tiny.

Fear galvanized him. His rolling gaze touched the Imperial Cluster and in a moment the ship was in incredible motion toward it. Jacarantha shrank behind them. For a few moments there was a blessed quiet.

"Two ships behind us," said Joquirl, murmuring.

Race saw them, ghostly in the fading sunlight. The instant he slowed they'd be alongside. He urged the ship to greater and greater speeds, until the stars flowed around them, streaked by and disappeared, but the gap never closed. He still felt them there. He visualized that gap growing larger; to no avail. *They* were visualizing it growing smaller.

Stop dead? No. They'd overrun, but not far enough to lose us. Change angle? No good unless their gyros are running. Besides, we'd get lost.

Second by second they left the stars he knew behind and fear swelled within him. Already he feared he was lost; leave this line and plunge into the unknown deeps?

The concentration that moved the ship, though intense, left him room for thought. "At least they're not shooting," he whispered, with effort.

"They can't," Joquirl murmured. "Nothing can exceed the speed of light. Technically our velocity is zero—we are traveling from point to point without crossing the space or time between, which means in zero time. We spend a minute fraction of a second in real space at each point, long enough to receive star-light and reflect it, but not long enough for light to cross from ship to ship. They can't radio us either."

None of which helped him. But he had come to a solution of sorts. Would he be able to fool *them?*

Mind firmly wrapped about his ship, he rehearsed his actions over and over, nodded in the light of the monstrously swollen Imperial Cluster that flooded the bridge. His forehead felt warm and odd.

In an instant he had stopped the ship dead and in another was in full flight backward—and in the third was fleeing at an angle to his former line of flight. For three seconds he held that angle, while several stars ticked past. If his change of angle went unnoticed—

He couldn't detect them. Presumably they couldn't detect him. He stopped. A second went by, then another. With a start he moved another marble from the pocket to the starboard firing port. Five seconds had passed.

Race took a long, deep breath and Joquirl also heaved a deep sigh when he saw that Race had relaxed. Touching his forehead, Race found that it was covered with sweat, not a film but an actual blister. The gentle air circulation had not been enough to detach it in free fall.

Blotting it he turned on the intercom. "Yale? Here's the situation. We were jumped by three ships off Jacarantha. I blasted one and the others chased us for—" he checked his watch—"ten minutes." *So long? No longer?* "We've just shaken them off—we think."

Even five seconds at those speeds would take him many times farther than they could search, if they lost him for an instant. Second by second his confidence grew.

"However, I'm exhausted. We may have to rest here while I sleep. I don't know how long. Better ration the water."

"Ben Perez here. Beggin' your pardon, Sir, there's no water except the boiler safety margin. Also, the battery charges are low, and the water purifiers are not in order. That means we're operating on the chemical air purifiers, Sir. Also, there's no spares for them—we'll have to shut down to bake'em—and the air tanks are empty. We can man the emergency generators, Sir, but they take almost as much air as they produce. Can you park us next to a star before you rest?"

"Yes—I should've thought of that. Tell me, are things as alarming as they sound? How much water can we tap from the boilers? Can we get the water purifiers working? In short, how long can we survive?"

"Till we run out of water, Sir. The water and air purifier is algae based—plants that make oxygen, Sir." Race nodded. *Dinine* had not had such elaborate equipment. "The algae stocks are gone. But if we have power, the chemical jobs will carry us for air. Can't say yet how much water the boilers 'ull take, Sir."

Race moved them to the nearest star—he remembered seeing it move just before stopping—and swung broadside on to it. The radiation sensors were still in place; they rated it as high in heat, low in light and UV; a small dim red sun. Presently Perez was calling to say that he was pumping water into the port side boiler tubes, then again to say that they had steam pressure. "The main generators are up voltage already. I'm piping spent steam over to preheat the starboard boilers, Sir. We should have seven or eight gallons of reserve—say thirty liters. One each. Remember, we may need to make up boiler leaks; we can't drink it all."

"How much can we condense out of the air?"

"We lose about a liter each per day by sweating and breathing, Sir—less for the kids. That's half the daily loss from all sources. We can't get it all back, either, and it won't be very palatable, Sir."

"So we have half a day's water reserve. Perez, make up a list of all the things this ship needs to be spaceworthy, in your department."

"Yes, Sir. Sir? Does the ship have a name?"

Long pause. *Ravenham? Jayce? Janinda?* They'd give leads to his origin, and were somehow inappropriate. "We'll call it *Nod.*"

"Yes, Sir."

"We can go several days without water, Sir," said Joquirl quietly when he had switched off.

"Some of those kids haven't had anything to eat since this morning. Yesterday morning. We've got to get in soon."

"Yes. I take it that we are lost? Sir?"

"Yes. I'm counting on you—and your reference books."

Joquirl pursed his lips dubiously. "I have a fair grasp of the theory of star navigation, but I've had no practice at all. And I notice that there seems to be not a single astrogational instrument in sight."

"They stripped it when they mothballed it."

Joquirl nodded, not quite looking at him. "If I may say so," slowly, "you're the strangest Starling I ever heard of. To be so ignorant—no offense intended, Sir—even at your age."

After a pause that seemed longer than it was, Race said, "I'm not—wasn't—a Starling. I was born a human peasant on a plantation. *They* kept me ignorant of practically everything. You know how even the best of *them* look upon humans.

You can bet they'd be less than overjoyed to meet a former human as an equal. Probably they'd just kill me."

"Ahem. I think not the best ... but many would certainly prefer to do so. However. ..." Joquirl sighed and looked at the Imperial Cluster. "I suppose we had better get busy. Fortunately you brought my notebook; it has protractors and straight edges. First we must identify the beacon stars about the Cluster. Umm ... there is the Milky Way, that black cloud is up, and the Cluster is north of the rest of the inhabited galaxy, so we want to go in *that* direction, roughly."

"How does that help us? We knew that."

"Our point of view could have been rotated. This also tells us on which sides of the Cluster to look for what beacon stars."

"How do we identify them?" Race asked, discouraged. "No spectro."

"By the angles. Ahem. If three stars of the proper color and magnitude are at the proper angles from each other, we'll know that they are the beacon stars we seek."

Race grunted. "The angles depend on where you are. If we knew where we were, we could identify the beacons; if we knew the beacons, we could tell where we are."

"You make it sound harder than it is," said Joquirl. In the face of an abstract problem, he had lost both his nervousness and his ineffectual air. He opened the reference astronomy and leafed through it, to a photo of the Cluster taken from somewhat closer than they were. The beacon stars were indicated, and once Race had turned the book to conform to the view outside, he located two stars that could well have been beacons.

"I didn't think it would be so easy!"

"It isn't, Sir. We must have three, and I prefer six. We must measure their angles to determine where we are, then travel in the indicated direction to place ourselves on the main traffic routes."

"Is that necessary?"

Joquirl paused, nodded. "I think so, Sir. Lacking astrogational instruments or really adequate references, we could easily be lost. At Neolan's distance, the Cluster's beacons aren't so easily distinguished. These periscopes are not highly telescopic."

"We'll have to buy some instruments, first chance we get." Race brooded a moment and said, "I've got to learn all the astrogation you can teach me and then some, but I have to think now. Go ahead and locate us."

"Very well, Sir."

Incredible that it had been only half an hour since

lift off from Jacarantha. Now that it began to seem that they were not badly lost, Race realized that reaching Mavia was not as simple as he had assumed. He had only been planning one step at a time—and Geremé Slavin had been keeping one step ahead of him.

What was he doing now? Having flushed him from Sonissa and tracked him to Jacarantha, Slavin had set a trap for him that had almost caught him. A sudden qualm went through Race as he realized that he was probably outlawed through all space. If his shot had been directed down and had struck the planet, awesome damage would have been done. Race had never heard of nuclear weapons; they'd been obsolete since the first Starling developed his latent powers. Whole planets had been bombarded to slag, the incident radiation all but sterilizing them, by pebbles or marbles flicked at them at nearly the speed of light. That was in the War Century, shortly after men boiled out from Earth, carrying with them the old human rivalries and hatreds.

Slavin would have a real crime to squash him for now. He had probably been in one of those ships—a one in three chance of his having been killed. Race didn't like the odds. The ships must have returned to Jacarantha by now. Slavin wouldn't hang around long. He'd have to talk to the S. Jacksons, they'd be furious and alarmed, but he'd cut that short and return to Mavia.

Probably on his way right now. To set another of his traps!

Race pondered. Surely the man must know by now that he was looking for Race Worden, not Hans Chen. Why, Roop and Firolla told him that. Of course Race Worden could have been a disguise—but Slavin would have checked on him as a matter of course.

Damn! That had never occurred to him before. He must have picked up Janinda and Jocela and grilled them about him. Race trembled at the thought. They might have spent days in some place like The Cup! His

urgent desire to get back to Mavia became a burning
need. Perhaps they were dead! Would Slavin cold-
bloodedly crush them lest they, too, develop Starling
powers?

Hell yes.

Even Norton Altamont might well approve. He'd
killed a Starling, left two humans to die in the wastes,
robbed others, interfered with justice and orderly society on Jacarantha, and shown a disposition to shoot
wildly when cornered. Altamont might prove as dangerous. A menace to human and Starling alike, the S.
Altamont would call him.

Slavin would bend every power of heaven and hell to
kill him. Mavia would be on alert as Jacarantha was.
More so. They'd watch every small ship. If he didn't
reply satisfactorily, he'd be blasted instantly. There'd
be a lot more than three ships, and every limb of the
globe would be watched.

Nor was that all. Slavin played a deep game. *He'll
set up another trap inside the first one.* Race's hunted
feeling grew. *They'll be watching everything!*

Wait. Starlings weren't *that* super. *He hasn't had
time to set up anything yet.* Nor would they all drop
everything for an indefinite time, to wait for him—blasted ship or no. *In fact, Geremé Slavin's the only one
who's even thought much about me. Well, there'll be
something like Sonissa's Committee of Public Safety
he'll report to. But I haven't seemed dangerous till
now—just another raffish Chen.*

Would Mavia's government know he was a former
human? *They may've been told, but I bet they don't
believe it.* He thought of Norton Altamont. Presumably
such men also ruled Mavia. *Probably Slavin didn't report that. Because it'd be a lot easier just to kill me
than to get men like the S. Altamont to agree that I
should be killed, before Jacarantha. They'd want to try
me for the death of that old Starling. Slavin wants to
kill me because I was human.*

He was sure of that. He had heard and read of Starlings who grew furious at the notion of equality or even degrees of freedom for humans—as if they could ever be truly equal or free when there were Starlings. Something in such men craved inferiors to exercise their emotions on. Even among humans, this taint ran deep. It seemed like years since Race had thought of the foreman, Keithly, on the Plantation.

Okay. He'll set another trap. Probably it's been set for weeks, if I got back to Mavia. If he knows anything about me, he won't waste his time watching the Plantation or the mountains. He'll know there's only one reason for me to go back to Mavia.

Race felt a sudden, poignant pang of loss. He could never go home again. Step by step, event by event, he had outgrown Mavia. All his efforts had been bent toward getting back—he had never thought beyond that. He shook his head, pulling himself out of that.

So Mom and Joss will be watched.

But no matter how closely they were watched, he *might* rescue them and get away. Slavin couldn't take the chance. *Why, they'd have to be free, loose, now!* His heart pounded at the thought. It had to be. How'd he ever find them if they were in a dungeon? *But no. Slavin would never turn them both loose.* Janinda would be free; Joss would be locked up. When he contacted his mother, word would reach Slavin and the trappers would be alert.

How do I contact her without them knowing?

A knocking at the locked bulkhead aft reached him faintly. He turned on the intercom. "What is it?"

"Food, Sir. Are you hungry?" A woman's voice, arch.

"Food? Where'd you find food?"

"Simmons found it, Sir. Part of the emergency reserve, he said."

Race unlocked the door, but when she had drifted past the Starling staterooms to the bridge he had second thoughts. "How much food was there?"

It was Allison Yale. She smiled at him. "Just a few

bricks, Sir. The rest went to the children and that poor Mr. Nekrasov who was so badly starved. Some of it was pretty moldy, but it's edible."

The portion she handed him consisted of two of the mealy bricks that were supposed to contain every essential element in the human diet, in proper proportions. One brick had been crumbled and apparently browned, then creamed into a kind of mush. The other had been sliced thin, into two-inch squares, and toasted. It smelled quite good and not at all moldy. *He* would have been given the very best. Each brick, he knew, massed 275 grams—weight, about ten ounces—one third of the normal daily minimum food requirement for a sedentary man. Heavy work would triple that.

Two bricks is two meals. They were very light meals; he had had no food in thirty hours. But there were children and genuinely starved men aft, and how long before they earthed again?

Allison caught the back of the chair and pulled herself toward him at an angle, in effect leaning over him, till her breast nudged his shoulder. "It's not bad at all, Sir," she said brightly. "I rather fancy myself as a cook. Not that there was much I could do with them."

Race had dated on Sonissa but always as a human; he had never had a woman, especially an older one, flirt with him. It embarrassed him and in a way it angered him—it was too servile. Didn't she have any self-respect?

The contracts of attractive young women on Jacarantha must be worth quite a lot. He had seen few of them on the streets.

"Do you want some?"

Joquirl had turned away and was bent far over his book. He shook his head without looking round, mumbling, "No, Sir, thank you, Sir. I had a good dinner, Sir." Giving them as much privacy as he could without ostentatiously withdrawing. Race ate slowly, carefully—his Starling powers helping to keep the mush in the bowl and the toasted wafers anchored. Allison continued to hover over him, almost continually in the intimate contact, speaking into his ear.

"Are we far from home? Is that the Imperial Cluster? Are we going there?" She did not babble—he gave her that—but was not really interested in the answers to her questions. Each answer was usually followed by an admiring or flattering remark. He kept his face turned as far away from her as he could. He was warm all through the ordeal.

When he had finished she lingered. "Shall I bring you more water, Sir? When do you wish to be awakened?"

Race's flush deepened, but he spoke evenly. "There won't be time to rest till we make planetfall, with the air and water situation as it is. That shouldn't be long."

When she left he tried to convince himself that she hadn't as good as made herself available. He knew, from reading and conversation, that Starlings often maintained human women, sometimes whole harems full. And Starling women often kept men. He had never fully realized, though, that the women could be eager for that kind of slavery.

Yet humans everywhere break their backs to get a chance to work for Starlings. They—we— are the source of all power and wealth. Of course they're eager—and proud when they succeed.

He thought of Yale as he had been in prison, a man among men. How would he take such a liaison?

Why, he'd be as polite and respectful as ever—wouldn't say a word. He would probably be glad of it! It's the best thing that can happen to a man, unless the Starling gets spiteful and kills him. The Starling would find some excuse to keep him around at good pay.

It shocked him to realize that many of the inequities were as much the fault of the underdogs as of the overlords.

"How's it coming?" he asked Joquirl, uncomfortably.

"Ahem. I think I have located us, Sir. We seem to

be west and above the main route to the Cluster from Finisterre. If we go *that* way—how far I have no idea—until these three stars are in almost a perfect equilateral triangle, we should be right on it."

Once he had the beacon stars pointed to him, Race could fly them by the seat of his pants. "Good. We'll be in air before we know it."

Perez wanted him to bring both boilers up to pressure, so they would have that much more steam to coast on between stars. Race rolled the ship over and in a short time they had pressure on both sides. Then he swung about and drove across the face of the Cluster at a fairly low speed, until the designated beacon stars formed a triangle.

While they were moving, he checked the index of the reference and pointed out the name of a planet: Chunder. "Plot us a course for this one."

Joquirl gave him an astonished look. "But that's in the Cluster!"

"Not deeply inside."

"There is no route to it, and it wouldn't be in this book if there was one."

There was no route to it because it was not inhabited. Once, it had been. It had been the capital of the Imperial Cluster and the staging point for the Hundred-Star Crown's attack on the stars outside the Cluster. Two hundred years ago there was a terrible battle which all but destroyed the planet.

The S. Starretts had begun the terraformation of it again, and after two hundred years it should be habitable, but the topsoil must be pretty thin. At least, the last thing Race had heard, there were no settlements.

"Why go there?"

"Water and algae. We can't be sure the algae is edible, but we don't care about that. As for food—I doubt we'll find any."

When they were on the traffic route between Finisterre and the Cluster, as nearly as they could tell with their protractors, Race turned *Nod's* nose until he had

the Cluster centered. As he drove toward it, it expanded; a hazy, luminous ball that spread half across the
sky, then two-thirds, then covered the wide-angle view
forward from side to side. Now, it was visible in the
edges of the side view.

"Chunder was near the old trade route in from Finisterre; that's why it was so important in the old days.
Now the routes have shifted." Joquirl muttered over
the reference book, peering hopelessly at the cloud of
light before and around them.

They felt their way down the traffic route, and finally Joquirl indicated a bright star. "Try all the stars
near that one—Chunder was near a very bright one,
too far inside the Cluster to be used as a beacon."

Race drove past the bright star, feeling hopeless;
there were five hundred stars within thirty light years of
him. But one by one he picked out the nearer stars,
eliminated those too large or small and red to be a normal planet's sun. Hours slid past while they drove past
star after star, looking for planets, examind the planets, rejected them, and went on. Once they found an inhabited planet, but they didn't stay long enough to find
out what one it was.

But at last they found it—about dawn by Jacarantha
time. Race was too exhausted to feel triumph, and
Joquirl was half-asleep. He brought them down by a
stream and a lake near a lofty range of hills covered
with pines. He went to sleep after telling Yale that the
crewmen had liberty.

It was late when he awoke, though the sun was only
halfway down the sky in the west. He had slept on one
of the sheeted beds in the Starling section, finding it
bare but for the spread, and dusty. Arising, he felt
dusty and musty himself, and he also felt the pressure
of time on him. *Should have gone straight to Mavia!*

But no, he'd decided that would do no good. He
couldn't get there before Slavin, and it would take him
time to find Janinda and Joss. The trap would be set no
matter how fast he moved. So there was no real hurry.

And we're in a damn dangerous ship. What's the point in saving them if we all suffocate together?

"Ahem. Sir, Mrs. Yale instructed me to tell you that your breakfast will be ready as soon as you awaken. Shall I notify her that you have awakened?"

The little man was apologetic about having spent the night in the Starling section, but Race was glad he had; if that bulkhead door had opened, Allison would have been in his bed.

"Yes, tell her. Wait a minute—the food should be saved for the kids." His hunger had awakened with him, and was stronger than he now, but that protest came automatically.

"I believe they have caught some fish in the stream, Sir. They're frying them outside now."

"Oh, fish. Okay, tell her. Have any of the people been attacked by any animals or anything?"

"No, Sir. There don't seem to be any animals."

Race looked curiously out at the planet. Unlike the planets destroyed in the War Centuries, Chunder had not been pounded until all its continental bedrock was pulverized and liquified, and its air glowing hot. Many places had not been struck at all. But when a marble or pebble entered the atmosphere at that terrible speed, several cubic miles of air were heated until it radiated in the X region. A single shot might sterilize a hundred-mile circle, even if the marble never touched the ground. Though many life forms could survive—and the seas would hardly be touched—these would be marginal forms, such as arctic or mountainous plants, that could not repopulate the devastated lowlands.

If the S. Starretts had not reseeded the planet, they might see nothing now but a sparsely-grassed, barren plain, shifting dunes or ridges of gravel, splintered bedrock, or once-molten stone; here and there a scrawny bush fighting to keep a toehold in the thin soil.

However, they *had* reseeded—re-terraformed is more accurate. The planet was left in a state almost as bad as a planet that had never known life, whose air was hydrogen, ammonia, methane, and carbon dioxide. Almost. The most that could be said for Chunder, after the last battle of the War for the Crown, was that its air was breathable and its water drinkable.

But a planet without topsoil is not habitable. Even now there was very little topsoil, Race decided. The grass seemed thin, patchy, to one used to the five-foot-deep topsoil of the Plantation of the Oroné. Except in the hills, which apparently had been protected by the trees then standing, there were no trees, and he guessed there wasn't soil enough for their roots. In the years after the battle, the winds and rains must have stripped every continent almost down to the broken bedrock Though a good farmer can add an inch of topsoil a year, Nature takes hundreds of years to build it up.

The cooking was being done down by the stream. There were a number of logs there, washed down from the hills—there was so little soil now that flooding was common. Most of his people were gathered in the shade of a couple of scrawny trees. He saw Allison's tawny-blonde mane approaching the ship with quick jerky steps, a platter in her hands.

Going to the lock on that side in the Starling section, he waved to her.

"There many fish there?"

"Seems to be quite a lot, Sir." She bent over him provocatively, but he ignored it as best as he could. "He took one of the dustcovers off the beds, Sir, and used it for a seine. They're just like the fish on Jacarantha!"

"They came from Earth, probably. Those are silverfish. Pretty small, though. They get twice as long as that."

She hung around and chatted, finding every excuse to bend over him, or face away from him. Race sat in the shade of the ship and sweated.

I've got to face it sooner or later. What am I going to do about her?

But making a decision was one thing, and implementing it another. Not only did he not want to hurt her feelings, but he realized that rejecting her would be humiliating and probably make an enemy of her.

He looked gloomily at Chunder. This might have been merely a wasteland on a desirable planet, the margin of a desert. But Starlings did not let land lie desolate. His knowledge that the whole planet must be like this troubled him. He kept remembering how Jacarantha had lit up in an instant from the flash of his shot—as Chunder had lit, so long ago.

He had the kind of powers that laid planets waste— and had used them once. Sitting there, scowling at Chunder, he let his mind drift back to his peasant days when the mere thought of Starlings had caused him to tense. He knew now that in every human sense they were no different from the peasants of the Plantation; he had not seen a single emotion or reaction among the S. Altamonts, or read of any in Starling novels that he had not seen in Ravenham.

That was the terrifying thing. Those stern, shining faces of his ignorant fancy might be unapproachable, but they covered minds that were just, fair, not swayed by emotion. *Better if they were really like that, even if I never could be.* This planet had been destroyed by Starling emotions.

I've got to watch myself. Mavia could wind up like this. It was this responsibility that he had feared, from the beginning.

Shaking off the mood, he stood up abruptly—Allison had fallen silent at his expression—and walked over to the stream. Silence fell as he approached the party, but they all looked happy, if a little apprehensive.

Yale met him. "This the planet where humans aren't registered, Sir?" He was wary.

"It is one, but not the one I was thinking of. We're here for water and algae, if Simmons can find anything suitable."

Startled at being singled out, Simmons hurriedly took a fishbone out of his mouth and said, "Yes, Sir. I've seen several clumps of algae. Any green goo will do, Sir. It doesn't really matter if it isn't edible."

"That's what I thought. I'd better move the ship down to the stream for the water—or should we take it from the lake?"

"I'd say the stream, Sir."

"Very well. It won't take the pumps long to fill the algae tanks. We should have plenty of sewage for it to work on, by now." He looked at the sky. Strange that the Cluster did not show, though he saw a bright point that was probably the beacon star Joquirl had indicated; those hundreds of stars did not pierce the hazy blue-green dome.

"I want to be out of here before night."

"Sir?" Yale was respectful. "Could you maybe help us catch fish? There's nothing to eat in the ship, and if this takes long—"

"Quite right. I'm not sure how much help I'll be, but I'll see what I can do."

It took longer than he had expected, because he had to take *Nod* up into sunlight to bring the boilers back up to pressure so that they might power the pumps. While they were pulling water up from the stream he considered fish. Flying over the stream and the lake he located many, including two schools. The water was silty with the erosion of the land, and the fish runty, but not bad-tasting.

After a little thought, he helped them spread several dustcovers across the mouth of a shallow cove. "We'll try to drive 'em in here and close it up after them," he said, and took up a couple of dead logs.

"I'll need help for this," he added, and picked out a red-haired girl at random, or nearly so. The seven crewmen were still very weak, their wives unsuitable for various reasons—he had no confidence in their judgment, and they might be frightened—and most of the children too young. Allison stood at a little distance, and she made him uncomfortable. But Pasy

Nekrasov was young, lively, intelligent, and so attractive that he had seen all her other qualifications.

He caught her up into the air and brought her to him smiling, but too shy to laugh. He put an arm around her to bind them into a single unit. She tried to act as if accustomed to this and to flying.

"You watch the fish on the right and let me know if they bolt back past us. I'll have to be handling two logs and can't see everything."

She murmured something and they went out over the lake. The shattered, treeless plain was hot and drab. This lake had once been a city; he saw shaped stone around it. He drove the logs gently down into the water, then moved them toward a school of fish broadside on. The noise alone would have startled them away, and there was no trouble until the water began to get too shallow for them.

Pasy squealed, gripping his collar with one hand and leaning to point with the other. Race churned the log in the water and turned the fish back, then had to do the same on his own side.

"Oh, they're going between the logs!"

Race churned the logs until two-foot waves arose, but many of the fish darted past their ends or even under them.

"It's like forking up soup!"

But many of the fish did run into the shallow cove. Instantly Yale ran out, waist-deep, bringing the dustcovers together. Race drenched him as he brought the logs up to the mouth, but Yale ignored that. He turned and draped the top of the sheet over the log, holding the bottom side taut. He was bent over despite the water splashing up into his face with each wave.

Ropy and several women followed more hesitantly, then Race had welded the logs and the spread dustcovers into a single flexible unit.

"Okay," he shouted. "I've got them! Stand by the shore and grab them as they come out."

He swept the fish farther into the cove with the improvised net, ignoring those who leaped over or dived under. Presently the surface of the cove was a seethe of leaping and swimming fish, and the humans were wading in with clubs and bare hands, tossing them far up on the shore, where the smaller children leaped and shouted and ran after them.

"This'll feed us for several days," said Yale, dripping but satisfied, as he looked over the mounds of silverfish.

"They'll have to be eaten quickly," Race said. "We've no way of sterilizing them."

His concentration had been too fierce for him to find time to put Pasy Nekrasov back on the shore; he had held her all through the clubbing. As he set her down now—less shy, she was in no hurry to leave his side— he glimpsed Allison Yale glaring at the girl.

At first he was innocently and honestly surprised, then for the first time since he saw Geremé Slavin he was genuinely amused.

13

While they hovered off Chunder to bring the boilers back up to pressure, Race had a fleeting thought of staying here, or heading for some planet in the Cluster before the news of the Jacarantha Incident preceded him, waiting a few weeks until the storm blew over. Even a grim manhunter like Geremé Slavin could only stay alert for so long.

But Slavin could outwait me easily. If he waited too long Joss and Janinda might be dead, or gone beyond his power to follow and find them, or changed out of all recognition. Perhaps worst of all: *he* might be changed too much, have grown beyond their capacity to follow. He couldn't bear to have Joss—and Janinda! —saying "Sir" to him.

They pulled out of the Imperial Cluster quickly and confidently and located the very bright star that was their target, next to the sun of Finisterre. Now real speed: at the same improbable speed that they had fled the local group, they returned. As it swelled before him and the Cluster shrank behind him to a hazy ball, he grew progressively more impatient. The ten minutes ticked past slowly, slowly.

Finally, the last few stars flashed past them. The target star flamed into horrendous size and stood there, just above the ship and blazing down on it. The radiation alarm clangored and he moved them away.

Now the Imperial Cluster was far enough away to be used as a single reference point. Joquirl spread his charts and quickly located the marked route to Sonissa. There was no direct route to small, obscure Mavia. Race followed him as he oriented himself against the Milky Way and the Cluster, and found the part of the skies that corresponded with the photo showing the direction of Sonissa's sun.

Then he picked out the beacon stars and pointed them out to Race. Knowing the right direction, he could fly it blind and possibly make it. But if he stopped confidently at a star and found that he'd wandered off the route, he could quickly get back on it by taking the angles of the beacons, which lay far off to right and left of his course. For this reason, star routes rarely went straight to the destination, but were made in short straight hops from one prominent star to another.

He had to fly blind, unable to see his destination. Sun-type stars are weak and inhabited planets scattered. But that did not matter. The route from Finisterre's target star to Sonissa was not more winding than usual, and there were only three target stars in it.

When he knew the direction, Race focused on the nearest bright star to the center of his forward scope and willed the ship toward it. Presently they streaked by it, but Joquirl already had the next photo ready. Race turned the ship slightly till the next target star was centered, then the next. Joquirl laid his protractor against the view aft, across Finisterre's target star and the center of the Cluster. When they had narrowed to the indicated angle, Race stopped.

There was no star near, but Joquirl was unperturbed. He had kept his eye on the beacon stars and now quickly located them, measured their angles as well as he could with his little protractor, and nodded. "It's somewhere very near us, probably one of the brightest stars in sight."

Race visualized the view just before he stopped. Four stars were moving swiftly across it. One was a red dwarf; another was orange. They had passed two lighter stars—Race located them. One was visibly brighter than the other. *Nod* plunged toward it.

It was the smallest star he'd ever seen, smaller than any red star. "A white dwarf," said Joquirl, interested, seeing for the first time some of the things he'd thought about. "Is there one near Sonissa?"

"I don't know."

The other star was quite a little distance back and off to the side, but it looked like a sun should. They streaked in, automatically looking for planets, and Race glanced at the Cluster to orient himself. He gasped in surprise and delight. It looked *right!*

Suddenly, overwhelmingly, the memory of his first starflight in the ill-fated *Dinine* returned. *Why, that little red star was the one we passed coming from Mavia!* He whirled *Nod* around and fled home. *Half an hour it took, first time.* He strained in concentration and did it in a minute this time. It was not possible to use the speeds he had used in fleeing the ships, because his concentration was broken by feeling anxiously ahead for the star, in readiness to stop.

Then they were there—he hoped.

Race oriented himself by the Cluster and Sonissa's star, and tried to remember what time of year it was. Let's see, it was going on three months since the Wordens had come to Middleport. It should be late winter or early spring. Knowing what time the Cluster rose at that time of year gave him roughly the triangle of Mavia, Sun, Cluster. So Mavia would be over *there. That's right. It's only going on seven weeks since I left.* It seemed years.

He sat frowning. He had had a couple of half-formed thoughts about the approach, and now, reluctantly, he developed them. The method scared him.

"There is an inner planet—small and airless—somewhere around here," he murmured, and spent several minutes driving past the sun on different sides until he had located it, as he had located Sonissa long ago. The inner planet, never named, had been the site of a battle in the old days, he recalled from his reading.

It was hot, and he had no idea of its rotation. Shrugging, he brought *Nod* down on a bleak, sun-blasted landscape at the terminator near the pole. He knew of the dangers of reflection; it was hotter here than in orbit. Landing on a ridge near the edge of the world, he put one of *Nod's* side boilers to the sun, leaving the other in shadow. At least they wouldn't get heat from both sides.

The crewmen looked up apprehensively as he flew through. He winced when Allison waved gaily to him, and pulled nervously away from the ports. Back in the holds, he looked thoughtfully at the S. Jackson personnel transport. It was made of tough, dense wood, glass, fiberglass, glassfoam, and the like. Its only metal parts were the generator and battery, the radio, and the wiring for the lights.

There were four holds, each ten feet high and with a separate hatch. But they weren't meant to open onto space; there were no locks.

Race measured the wagon's width with a piece of wire. It would fit the central passage through the crew's quarters from bridge to holds. But there was a turn. . . . Bringing the wagon after him, carefully, he examined the cross-corridor forward of the crew's quarters, on the bottom level—the keel deck. It ran from an airlock on one side to another on the other side, with doors opening into various parts of the crew compartment. Forward of it was the sealed bulkhead of Starling country.

Measuring the airlock on the shaded side of *Nod*, Race was relieved to find it large enough. He had only to bend the long wagon around that right angle, from the central passage to the cross-corridor. He studied the wall. It looked like wood but felt like glass; his Starling sense told him it was vitrified wood—soaked in a silicone solution that was polymerized to form a glassy sheath around every fiber and cell. It was theoretically airtight against emergencies, inch-thick slabs closely pinned to a heavy framework of vitrified beams slung between two monstrous beams at top and bottom.

Race pulled away the sheathing in large slabs—it was tongue-and-groove—and laid it by in order. The studs, close-set four-by-fours that had to carry the monstrous weight of air pressure if the locks failed, were notched and dowelled into the under and overhead beams. With half a dozen of them out—he had to spring the beams apart with vast creakings—and Yale's help. He turned the wagon into the passage. Then, painstakingly, he rebuilt the wall.

There was nothing to say. He shut the door, hoped the wall was airtight, and shrugged. Opening the inner door of the airlock, he squeezed into the wagon—the door would only open a crack and for a moment he thought his plan would founder.

Twisting the spill valve, he listened as the air shrieked out past the reeds that shrilled in alarm. On the dash before him was an ordinary flight radio, a magnetic compass, a wind-speed indicator, and a glass pyramid usually called a pressure cock or airbird. It was partly full of a cheerful bright blue liquid, freezeproof; when the liquid climbed up into the peak, the air pressure had fallen below safe limits.

It was the cheapest kind of barometer, but not one that would be used in a high-altitude car, much less a spaceship. Often, Starling air vehicles were spaceproofed—*not* space worthy—adequate for a short hop to a moon or satellite. Even a low-level, short-haul workhorse like this might need to go half around a planet quickly, by suborbital flight. If it could tolerate vacuum for even one minute—

Impatiently, he seized the thick quartzfoam door with his Starling power and pulled it gently toward him. Air shrieked out past it and the wagon edged forward; before he could stop it, the gale was gone and a vast silence sat on him. The liquid blue deathsign hadn't moved.

He glanced at his watch, waited, waited, peered at

the airbird. Now he saw a fine base mark scratched in the glass. The blue was—wasn't it?—a notch above it. More seconds ticked past. It was definitely above. He couldn't see it move, but at the end of a minute it was a full two millimeters above the mark.

Since the neck narrowed, the second minute would show a gain of at least four, he estimated. The third minute would see a gain of a full centimeter; the fourth, to the top. After that, they might have another minute.

He shut the door, trying not to shiver—he hadn't even noticed the blasted black lands beyond—and opened the door in the corridor a crack. Air howled in, ghostly at first, gradually filling the corridor. Race backed the wagon till its door coincided with the other and stepped into the crew's wardroom.

Most of them were here. Two of the children stopped jumping up and down in the low gravity as he appeared and said, "Fetch the others." When all were with him, Race spoke slowly.

"You all know that I promised to take you to a planet where humans are not registered and where you will have a fair chance to be happy. We're not far from just such a planet now, one you'd all like—I know it well. But we're not there. I'm wanted by authorities there and we'll be watched for in the worst way. The only way in is to go in the flying wagon. That's dangerous in itself; if they spot me, they'll blast me without a chance to do anything. If that happens, anybody who stays behind will die very shortly; no one will know they're here."

He looked them over solemnly, counting them. "I'm not giving you a choice. Better to die quickly than slowly. Pack up a few things you can carry and get in the wagon—all of you." Deliberately he added, in a wry tone, "I'll keep my promise or die trying."

That produced a surprisingly hearty laugh; the beaten slaves of the S. Jacksons had come alive enough to appreciate gallows humor.

"Joquirl, Yale, Perez, Simmons, up in the flight offices."

When they were settled he said, "Do you have that list I asked for?"

Perez nodded eagerly and handed him a grimy piece of paper covered with the neat printing of those to whom writing is a tool much like arithmetic.

> Algae yeast
> Water air
> Food bricks
> Space suit
> Steamfitter's kit

They could never bring all that back in the wagon. Race frowned. "You want the regular edible algae. Right. What's it like?"

Simmons, who was the specialist in air/water said, "In the light tanks it's the usual green goo." Algae required light. "They sell it in dry powder form, in ten-star packages, like yeast." He seemed to notice nothing odd in a Starling's ignorance of it.

Race knew yeast; it was sold in, as he said, hundred-gram packages. "How much?"

"I'd want ten packages to get started, and twenty or thirty for safety. It doesn't keep for more'n five, six months, Sir."

Like yeast. "Okay. Why yeast?"

Simmons cleared his throat importantly. "Well, Sir, the algae has to have carbon dioxide, and if there's a sudden change in personnel levels, it won't get enough and will start to die back, which'll put a stink into the air. So we dump sewage or usually algae into a dark tank with yeast. See, the sewage is boiled before the algae even get at it, sterilized. The yeast feeds on the algae and generates carbon dioxide. We can harvest it—it's edible—and can it. *Nod* carries six ten-liter canisters for yeast."

"Not much of a reserve, but we can always grow

more. I see. Yeast comes in about a hundred flavors, if I remember rightly. Water—we already have that. *Nod* is equipped to distill it for the boilers?" Perez nodded.

"That gives us a boiler margin too, then. Air has to be pumped in at a port. Ships don't carry air pumps." Race frowned. The provisions for emergency seemed scant; *Nod* was meant to operate close to space ports, on a regular schedule. What he really wanted was a pioneer ship, designed to be self-sufficient and capable of years of sustained flight.

He didn't have time to follow that up. Perez cleared his throat. "We could run a pipe from the airlock pumps to the reserve tanks. Take a long time to fill'em up, though."

That was something, granted the air. "Space suit. Yes." There should be at least one, in case something should go wrong outside, say with the boilers. "We do have spare boiler tubing and steam pipes?"

"Yes Sir, a full complement, I think."

"Well, things are not too bad." Race handed the list to Joquirl. "We'll need a complete set of astrogating instruments—telescopes, spectros, sextant, course cameras especially—and full references for the local group and the Imperial Cluster."

"The last may not be available, so far away." Joquirl took the list and turned it over to write on the back. "We'll need playbacks for the cameras."

If they had had course cameras they'd never have gotten lost, though they were no help in getting to a place where they had never been before. One sat in the bow and recorded the view forward, the other in the stern and recorded the view aft, on magnetic tapes. These could be replayed, backwards, on a TV tube, so that the ship could thread its way back between the stars to its starting point.

"Now. I want to leave the ship with steam up, and I think we'd better cross-connect the boilers, so that the tubes on the dark side can radiate away some of the excess heat. It'll be hotter than hell in here in a week, even so."

They nodded but Perez pursed his lips. "If the system springs a leak anywhere, she'll bleed dry."

Yale was frowning intently. "You don't intend to stay on—Mavia? Sir? You going to take us with you?"

Race looked at him. "I can't stay." His voice was dry on the words. "It wouldn't be safe for any of you, either. Jacarantha is only two stars away, and there's going to be a lot of talk about this. They'll hear you're on Mavia and demand you back. But nobody has to come with me unless he wants to."

Yale's frown deepened, but Perez and Simmons looked relieved. Race counted his humans to be sure that all were in the wagon, and stepped into the glass-walled cabin.

Ready? His heart raced, he gulped for breath, his knees were weak. But it was the only way. He opened the inner and then the outer lock, slid the wagon forward. There was an agonizing moment as it scraped past the eighteen-inch-thick lock doors, then they were outside, in the shadow of *Nod* and the ridge. Both were edged with hellfire.

He shut both lock doors, made sure they were tight. The corridor was left in vacuum, but would probably leak full in a day or so. The blue liquid had not moved visibly. Race glanced around the sky: Mavia was beyond the ridge. They would pass the sun going away, on their left. He rotated the wagon until the sun was under their feet and the planet below their right sides—the airbird's head was instantly flooded, but it was worthless in zero gee anyway.

Then the sun leaped up all around the windows from the pit below them. It *was* hellfire. It *squirted* past the wagon. Its glare off the windshield all but washed out the stars. The air heated up as if a blow torch brushed across them.

But they were leaping away from it even before Race lined them on Mavia. He could not use his full speed for fear of overrunning it, but the little wagon handled better than the ship. It was not a matter of mass, but of size; he gripped it more readily. Even he was amazed at the speed of that crossing; he'd estimated a minute at the outside, not less than thirty seconds.

In five seconds Mavia had grown from a bright star to a small disk and was rapidly becoming a globe. The first five seconds carried them two-thirds of the distance; the second took them the rest of the way. It being winter, the north pole was toward the sun. To avoid the radiation belts, as he must in this thin-walled craft, he must dive down the polar chute. He aimed for the northern limb, just above the great white storm whirl, to miss the atmosphere.

The second five seconds were an age. He had had an image of Starlings in ships and satellite-tracking stations, firing ports readied, each scanning his sector of the sky. Then he had had a more realistic picture of humans manning the scanners, with Starlings on alert but relaxed. Then he had had a still more realistic image of computers doing the scanning, with Starlings in the background, and maybe humans. Only computers could deal with Starling speeds.

In any case, even the first, he would have seconds to make the approach. In the latter case, the computers might well ignore him. He knew that his speed was well above light on the first part of the hop; crossing the space close to the planet he should be very near it on the average, slowing as he approached the planet. Thus the *first* images the computers would receive of him would be from near the planet—then the farther echoes would come in.

Battle computers, if the programs survived from the wars, would alert at the signs of such speed. But if the computers weren't "battle-trained", they'd think he was *leaving*.

Nevertheless, he felt horribly unprotected as the wagon came to a halt over the white swirl at Mavia's pole. Stopping was a wrench, like waking out of a nightmare, but the nightmare went on and on.

Air—how much had they lost? The airbird was worthless since he had tipped the nose up, despite its baffles, worthless in no-gray anyway.

Radiation—how much had they taken from the sun and the radiation belts?

The Starlings—second by second he was amazed that he had not felt that final flash of intolerable heat (hellfire cubed), though he realized feverishly that they'd never shoot so near the planet—

The Starlings again—had they been detected? Had Mavia become a giant trap he could never escape?

Then the propeller on the nose—he was diving nose down—began to spin in air and he slacked off the furious dive. *Slowly now, slowly.* Air was still too thin for the air-speed indicator to read true. The propeller that drove the generator was triple, a small highspeed cone in the middle, successively larger props behind it, on concentric shafts. At first only the inner one spun; then as air grew denser and their speed fell off, the two larger ones came on, clicking as they unfeathered. They were down, and the air was bitterly cold.

14

Allison Yale woke him. Race came out of an eon of sleep slowly, anguished. Somewhere back down there, Joss was drowning. He had pushed her in—it was an impulse, sudden and irresistible—then she was carried away from him despite his struggles to get to her and save her. His struggles took *him* farther away—

The anguish faded and he realized it had all been a nightmare—they were in the Mountains of the Oroné and he was in the tent, his mother bending over him. He smelled meat grilling.

Then he was awake and it was all true, even the drowning. It was a brassier blonde than his mother who bent archly over him with a bowl of stew. He sat up slowly, conscious of his bare chest, of the fact that her coarse blue shirt was unbuttoned at the top.

"Morning, Sir! Lovely day. Oh, a lovely planet, a wonderful planet, Sir!"

As if I had invented it. It occurred to him, irrelevantly, that if he took her into his bed, she would still continue to call him "Sir", never by his name. Always, he shied away from such thoughts. Now, near again to his mother more so than ever.

They were on Mavia, in the Mountains of the Oroné, and he *was* in the tent. Allison had appropriated the best of the furs for him, though he had ordered them reserved for the kids. He had been too tired to notice when he went to sleep. By the time he had located himself by navigation satellite and taken a suborbital flight to the right continent, and found the Mountains of the Oroné and their cache, he was exhausted. It was mostly the tension. Fortunately, it was only a little after dark by local time when he had moved them northwest to an unfamiliar part of the mountains. He had picked up a deer and warned them not to build a fire in the open, where it might be seen from orbit, then had plunged into sleep.

Now he frowned as he thought of all the things he must do this day. They had some bedding, but not enough even with the Wordens' furs; the tent was adequate for only two or three. They had his grandfather's rifle and a few shells, but none of the Jacaranthans knew how to shoot, nor would meat alone be adequate. He was flat broke.

"How long are we going to be here, Sir?"

Race grunted in ill-humor. "Too long." Allison fell briefly silent, made a couple of tactful comments and, to his relief, left him.

When he came out, word that he was in a bad mood had already spread. The laughter was hushed and the men glanced at him guiltily. He saw women shushing children, saw the children glance quickly at him and go blank-faced. It made him angry, uncomfortable as always, and he frowned.

They were in the lower foothills, north of the mountains, protected from the worst of winter's winds. But it was still very early spring and the nights were chilly. Race located a slab of bedrock near the surface, broke it off, raised it up trees and all, then started slicing thick blocks off it with wire he had found in the ship. Starlings commonly carried fine, heat-resistant wire in their work vehicles for shaping stone or wood. The blocks he stood on edge in the pit under the elevated slab—he smoothed the floor first—making walls. Onto them he lowered the slab, having elevated it about two meters.

Probably will flood in the first rain, but it'll do for a camp.

Race did some fine work to make a door and steps down to it, then cut two holes in the roof, lifting the dirt out above them. Making two tubes of stone, he set them into the holes in the dirt, on the slab; two more tubes reached up to the hole from the floor. Two fireplaces were built up around these tubes.

He finished by flying around over the hills collecting dead tree trunks and several green ones, rapidly splitting them up into large and small logs. One wooden slab he shaped into a thin but heavy door, which he leaned against the door-opening, lacking any way of hanging it. As a final touch he cut a window in one slab of stone, parked the wagon before it, and turned its headlights on.

The job took about an hour, and his people had stood around watching with the wondering and delighted eyes of children.

Race was in a better mood though valuable time had passed, feeling well enough to bear the delighted babble of Allison Yale and even the proprietary way she patted him on the shoulder before them all. With a few brief words of instructions he waved to them and flew off.

The Mountains of the Oroné ... so at last he had come home. Hunted, in desperate plight, half in despair over his mother and sister, but home. As near and as much at home as he'd ever be again.

This is probably my last visit to Mavia—ever, he mused, drinking in the craggy heights, the pines, the wheeling birds, and above all the rich, glorious green sky of home. Nostalgia was an ever-sharp pain in him. Each opening of the mountains into a new valley, each new sweep of pine-clad slope or clean flow of snow, was a pang.

Everywhere he expected to see traces of their old camp—had it only been three months since they fled the winds of winter from these very mountains? *If only Joss and Mom were with me this one last time!*

That brought back his sense of urgency. Trying to ignore the yearning spell of the slopes, he concentrated on finding gold, sweeping patiently up and down the valleys. Whenever he spotted dust in the stream bed, or in the bottom where a bed had once been, he scoured the slopes above to find the pocket from which it came.

Despite himself, he kept watching for traces of their old camp. It was a hundred miles southeast of him now, but the mountains looked just the same here as there. His sense of urgency also kept him watching for Spires—some of the Oroné lived in the mountains. More likely, he corrected himself, maintained seasonal residences. They'd be empty now. *But if we were spotted coming in, Slavin might know enough to patrol the Mountains. . . .*

He kept watching the sky, drinking in its color, but saw nothing but birds. Near evening he had accumulated about half a kilogram, fifty stars, of gold, and a deer. His powers were better trained now. *It won't buy all we'll need, but—*

"Mavia is a small planet," he said quietly to Joquirl and Yale. "There are only a couple of thousand Starlings here, not counting unpowered children. Most of the young ones leave. Astrogation instruments probably aren't made here. Most other space supplies probably are, but they aren't often sold. For a strange Starling to walk in and start asking for steamfitter's tools, space suits, even food bricks, would be a giveaway. Geremé Slavin knows perfectly well that *Nod* was mothballed."

"Meanin' we can't equip, Sir?"

"Yes. But some things we can get. Yeast, for instance—hunters' and campers' yeasts are the same as ship yeasts. Food bricks, even, might be needed by a human. Steamfitter's tools could be bought. And the reference books could be—you could say you were an instructor at the academy."

Joquirl cleared his throat. "You propose to take us with you?"

"Yes. But first I've got to change this gold."

Taking the wagon, Race made a quick trip to a town near the headwaters of the Amaranth. Here, he posed as a Starling on a camping trip. His bright clothes, wilted after days of wear, had been washed while he was asleep—more of Allison Yale's wiles. His work during the day had not soiled them. His fifty gold stars almost broke the bank, and he had to take 200 silver stars in change, which suited him.

He bought blankets, two ten-kilogram sacks of flour, a couple of bushels of vegetables, sheets, and towels, in the hasty, careless manner of a hurried Starling in his late teens, who knew little of cooking and living arrangements.

"Hurry, or I'll miss the party."

They hurried and he was back in camp before sunset. He hurried Joquirl and the three Yales through another meal, instructed Perez and Simmons briefly in the use of the rifle, and was relieved to find that Nekrasov's two sons had brought in a string of fish. They'd get by.

The sun had not yet set in Bridgetown when Race eased the wagon to the ground in the declining Mountains of the Oroné above it. He lifted a slab and contrived a hangar much like the camp house, but with no opening a man could crawl through. Then he flew them down to a road not far from the city. Fortunately, trees grew up to and into the city.

"I'm too well dressed to associate with you," he said. "Too well dressed to be walking the roads from outside the city. You go on in and make for the riverfront on Port River. Look for the Arlen Transport Company, with engines and offices in scarlet and violet, when you have bought your new clothes. I'll be in shortly after dark."

Less than an hour later they were on a passenger barge, bound upriver for Middleport. All day, in the mountains, Race had felt Joss and Janinda to be near him. It was as if the months had been a dream and their memories, that had faded into worrisome and persistent ghosts, had bloomed into fully-fleshed individuals again. At every moment he had felt that he'd hear them call laughingly to him as so many times before, that he'd fly over a hill and see the old camp high in the mountains and them by the fire. He was glad it had been dark and he had been half asleep when they opened their cache last night.

Now he remembered poignantly that first ride up the Port River; the sounds and smells, the bells and the laughter of the barge train brought it all back. It amazed him to find that it was an incredulous Hal Yale, a happy Allison, and an almost tearful Joquirl who were behind him. The Yale boy was as wide-eyed as his father. They arrived at Middleport shortly after midnight and spent the rest of the night in the depot.

The next morning, Race gave the Yales and Joquirl more silver than they had ever owned at once in their lives, and their instructions. The Yales were to wear their Jackson blues and make the rounds of the cheaper boarding houses, registering at each one if necessary, until they found where Janinda Worden was staying. (Allison frowned at this other woman's name.).

They were to claim to be from the Plantation of the Oroné and when speaking to her, they were to ask her if she wasn't the daughter of Jayce Sturtevant. (Sturtevant was his mother's maiden name, but he did not tell them that.) Whether the answer was yes or no, they were to say that they had met Sturtevant in Riverside Park about sundown.

"That should be all that's necessary. Whatever you do, don't underline it; don't keep hinting. Just keep it a sort of make-conversation thing—especially if there's anyone else in hearing. And don't say it more than once, even if she acts like she didn't notice you'd said anything important. Because she won't."

Allison said brightly, "Okay, Sir. That's easy enough; we won't let you down." But Yale's grim nod meant more to him. Again, he was bemused at this loyalty in the face of his wife's unconcealed betrayal.

When they had gone, he said to Joquirl, "You'll have plenty of time to take a room at the Port Barracks—the old barracks were turned into a middle-class apartment house for humans—and to buy the books. You're teaching at the Rosemont Academy here—it teaches humans, but they learn astrogation so they can teach it to Starlings.

"Tonight you'll be in Riverside Park, watching for Janinda. You have her description? There may be a girl with her. If not, ask her: *where is Joss?* Don't introduce yourself as Sturtevant, but don't deny it if she asks you, or if she asks if you represent Sturtevant. Let her know your address but not mine; tell her we'll be in touch with her. Make it brief and completely casual. She's almost certainly being watched, so be careful; don't let them get onto you. Telephone me at the Spanish Casa afterward—make sure no one's close enough to see you dial or hear you—and tell me the answer to the question. I'll register as, um, Arlen Peebles."

He expected Joquirl to ask him if this was his mother, but the old man surprised him by clamping his mouth firmly shut and imitating Yale's determined nod.

Race's own schedule called for little to do. He bought the protein-rich yeasts carried by hunters, food packaged for them, not as compact but more appetizing than the bricks, and the steamfitter's tools. He stored them in a port warehouse in a couple of shipping containers. By sundown he was hovering over his phone—the Casa was quite expensive, but had privacy—his belly knotted in agony and anticipation. When it rang it frightened him, as meeting Geremé Slavin suddenly might have done.

Joquirl's voice was even. "Joss is in Slavin Towers." *Click!*

Race sat down slowly, hung up. His knees were weak with relief. He had not been able to believe it would really work. This itself might have been a trap—it might not have been the real Janinda—and Joss might not really be there, even if it *was* Janinda.

But, he was sure, *Slavin would never believe I'd think ahead and plan this carefully, after all the flatheaded things I did in the past.*

Slavin Towers? *That's here in Middleport—at least he didn't take her half around the world. But it's meant for a trap, not to keep her away from me.* Then he remembered that the Towers was a residential spire— not an official one.

It was seconds before the realization came to him: he had taken her into his home. At first, it shocked him that Janinda would allow such a thing. He was so angry, mostly at Slavin, that it was many minutes before he could see it from their side.

Item: they had had no way of knowing whether he was alive or not. They might well have been told he was dead. Janinda would never believe that he would abandon them. Neither would Joss.

Item: Joss had already been sold into more degrading bondage. True, that was for a purpose. But Janinda might have avoided it; they could have waited, gone back to the mountains for gold to buy his way in, or just studied books to get the knowledge he had had to have.

Item: they had known he was in trouble, if alive. He might be years in returning; and in years passed as a Starling, he might well outgrow them. Ordinary human success alone could come between a man and his family, after all.

Could they really believe I'd forget them? Reluctantly he decided that Janinda, that monument of calm acceptance, could do so; could have done so. The agonizing thing was that she wouldn't have blamed him; she'd have gloried in his success and asked nothing more for herself.

Joss would've been bitter, though. He agonized over what she must have thought of him, to do this. *But what else could she do?*

Joquirl had enough time to get back to the Barracks. Race called it, had him called to the phone, spoke briefly. Through the Yales, he was to tell Janinda to come to "Peebles'" suite at the Spanish Casa immediately. (*No matter if she's followed; Slavin will be too busy to answer the phone!*) The Yales were to assemble with Joquirl. They, too, were to join him immediately. If he wasn't in, they and Janinda were to meet him where the flying wagon had been hidden; wait there for him for three days, after which, they were on their own.

Race had bought more clothes for himself, including a dark suit he donned now. He left the Casa by his window, arrowed straight up from its roof until he was above the glare of the street lights.

Slavin Towers was not one of the highest spires, about six hundred feet, out on the edge of the bowl valley. He hovered, looking it over. Its top was crowned with a building like—a coronet, was the best description Race could think of. He had never dreamed of such things as castles, and the only fairy tales he'd heard or read dealt with Starlings in a Starling world. The slender towers rising from the curved roofs reminded him of some lush flower, and he scowled at the thought. The place had all the marks of a harem. It was not lit up, though it was only an hour after sundown. His scowl deepened.

If Slavin was alert, it would be impossible to approach undetected. He'd be sensed seconds away. The only approach that might shield him would be to come up from below, close against the shaft. Its mass should screen him. But as soon as he came up to the level of a door, he'd be detected. Slavin might not be so alert. No one could be on guard all the time. But the other had had three days in which to rest from his chase.

Still, even if he believes I'm on the planet, after three days he can't be really alert. Say we were detected coming in. Even so, he can't—I hope!—know I've found out where Joss is. Surely he had received no warning from the Janinda-spies.

Race fell soundlessly, the cool night air flowing around him, and rose slowly, slowly, up the shaft. Nearing the top, he practically crawled, hands against it. He stopped with head against the bottom of the building.

Some spires were flat-topped, the buildings set on a disk balanced upon them. But most were like the Towers, the shaft blossoming wide at the top, with flying buttresses reaching out gracefully to take the load. That created basements.

It made his work harder; there was too much dead space and mass between him and the upper, inhabited parts of the building. But Race slowly went around and around the shaft, controlling his urgency, until he had surveyed all of the building he could.

There's no one home!

Since the population of Starlings on Mavia had declined after the war years, near-empty spire buildings were not unusual. But one that was being inhabited should have had servants—and the one inhabited by Geremé Slavin would have had a lot of girls in residence, if no other servants.

That just proves it's a trap, though.

He needed no proof. Cautiously, he raised his head above the lip of the edge. The Towers had no perimeter balcony at "ground" level, but there was a railing around the roof to keep babies from falling off. He concentrated his Starling sensitivity on the towers, one by one. *No. No one was in them.*

That left the main building. Race inched his way up until he could see the formal garden on its roof, around the towers. There were too many rooms, too much mass, for him to check without going over the roof, which would expose him to detection. But study of the building, and thought, led him to them. He deduced which were the main lounges, dining rooms, etc., and by elimination, which were the bedrooms.

It was the latter he checked. Just off the master bedroom, which had a floorspace equal to the whole ground floor of their house in Ravenham, was a cosy little room. In it were two people, facing each other across a table. Race crept closer and probed every room around it for hidden men.

He's alone! They might be hidden out of sight, but they couldn't be too far away. A Starling's powers were not very effective, except when he could see what he was doing.

Why, that means he doesn't know I'm on the planet! He may believe I am, but he couldn't get anyone else to. To capture a Starling, two or more others had to overpower him; a simple two-face duel was too chancy. It was not a question of one Starling having more power than another, but quicker wits, more tricks or training, or a better understanding of the other's mind. Bluff and psychology counted.

His trap is still set, though—alone. Oh, of course; Geremé Slavin could never doubt his ability to face down a human, even one with Starling powers.

Race hesitated, coping with his own long-fought fears: could he face a Starling? He had never confronted one as a Starling himself. *—And in combat too!* But he had no choice, nor any time to dither over it. The compelling need to get Joss out of there *now*, fly her and their mother to the wagon and off the planet before it was alerted, pulled him on. And the old fears paled under that urgency.

Race traced the shortest route to that small room. Under the ground floor level he crept, until he was opposite the door nearest it. Taking a deep breath, he bounced up and flung it open.

Every light in the castle flamed on.

15

Starlings didn't ordinarily need burglar alarms, but Slavin was ingenious. Cursing himself for not having gone through a window, Race hurtled through a room and down a corridor. The next opened just before he got to it. With a thrill of fear he slammed to a stop in the corridor and plunged through it.

Geremé Slavin stood smiling before him, wearing a gold-velvet dressing gown and shingle-sequined sock boots. Slender, elegant, shorter than Race, his olive skin as smooth as a child's, his black hair beautifully waved, his black eyes gleaming. His handsome face lit with pleasure as he nodded to Race.

"Race Worden, late of the plantation of the Oroné, come for your sister, I presume."

Race was breathing too hard to answer, though he had flown in. Nor did he feel like it; he knew better than to bandy words with this man. This wasn't the cosy little room they had been in; that was two rooms away yet, in the same bedroom suite. This was a morning room—he didn't have time to look at it and was only vaguely conscious of its restrained elegance.

His lips peeling back from his teeth, he tried to let go of the two marbles clenched in his right hand. His fingers wouldn't move. No part of his body would move. It was like when he was trying to open the gap between *Nod* and the S. Jackson ships and they were trying to close it; their efforts nullified each other.

In a Starling duel there were two basic ploys: to hurl

176

the enemy against something solid to "squash" him, or to hurl something *at* him. The two defenses were equally simple: to freeze one's body in position, holding it there by mind, and to freeze the positions of everything within range. This last was done by expanding the mind to include everything around, as in driving a starship.

They stood more motionless than statues that vibrate to ground tremors, smile and snarl frozen on their faces. Actually, each retained effortful control over his body—the other could not visualize it in as great detail—but neither was attempting to move. Race's breath came slowly; his lungs and diaphragm would scarcely expand. His heart throbbed irregularly and before he had consciously realized it, his mind had taken hold of it and grimly measured out its beat.

Race felt something move behind him and froze it. He tried to pick up the corner of the rug behind Slavin, but it rose only an inch. The eyes of a marble head beside Race suddenly leaped out at him, but he stopped them within a foot of himself. They hung there, one more thing for each of them to concentrate on.

Each new attack and its repulsion was made by conscious concentration; as soon as that situation stalemated, the unconscious took over, holding the attack or repulsion in place. There is a distinct limit to the number of things a man's mind may hold, nor is it the same for all men. The end of the duel would come when one of their minds was overloaded.

But duels are usually ended by tricks, Race thought effortfully. *Where's his trick? Didn't he think he'd need one?*

To force him to spring it before his mind overloaded, Race sent his concentration deep into the ground, gripped the bottom of the shaft, shook it.

It moved!

Slavin caught it on the second wobble, glared at him as things tumbled to the floor elsewhere in the castle. *He wasn't expecting that!* It made things more difficult

and dangerous for Slavin; if Race shook down half of
Middleport, the Planetary Council would be furious at
him, whether he caught Race or not.

Slavin began firing things at him in earnest, one every second or so. To do this he had to release his previous attacks, one by one; but Race did not detect the
deception for several seconds. When he did, he was angry at himself. The instant he had stopped one of the
other's attacks, he had begun to visualize the object in
that place. Naturally, he couldn't tell when the other
man had released it.

But he can't be pressing any *of his attacks, then!*

His only trick was to overload Race. Realizing that,
Race abandoned all of his own attacks to spring his
own trick. The marbles he had brought with him were
a blind. In his belt was a small brass grommet around a
hole. This he had loosened, not that that was necessary.

But before he could move it, a whimper distracted
them. With the intensification of the duel both had narrowed their concentration to this room. Now, Geremé
Slavin twisted his head painfully to smile reassuringly
at Joss.

Her face was twisted with anguish and she was raising a pistol. Instantly, Race's tiny brazen missile sped
toward the other's chest. Slavin stopped it a yard away,
automatically, but in the same instant the bullet sped
toward him.

Both Starlings felt the bullet before they heard the
bang, but Geremé Slavin made the mistake of gripping
it as if it were propelled by a mind, not merely flung at
him. He should simply have deflected it. Consciously
gripping two objects at once was too much even for
him, and one was controlled; the grommet broke loose
and in a moment had stitched through him twice.

The agony blinded him and broke his concentration.
Instantly, Race's two marbles struck him with soft
thumps. Hysterically he churned them about in the
other's chest.

Pink foam burst from Slavin's nose and mouth with

a groan and he toppled at Joss's feet. Panting, Race ran forward, forgetting the dying man.

Joss's hands were over her face and she had turned away immediately after the shot; she had seen nothing of that terrible death. Race crowded her back into the doorway, blocking her view. Her eyes were wide and unseeing.

"Oh, I killed him, I killed him." It was a moan, from so deep down that she could not cry.

Race, who was viciously glad, on a deep level, that Slavin was dead, never noticed the depth of her anguish. His own sense of triumph was instantly buried under two emotions: concern that she not see him, and the awareness of the passing of time. He had to clean up the mess.

"Wait here—this won't take but a minute," he managed to say, and shut the door.

Slavin was dead, an unpretty sight. Heartbeat, none; expression locked in incredulity, staring eyes fixed on the door where Joss had stood. *He never believed she'd shoot at him! And he knew she was my sister!* No time now to ponder Starling egotism. Race seized a small, deep-piled rug with his mind and turned it upside down to blot up the blood, finished by lifting the body and winding the rug around and around the head and shoulders. There were still stains.

Joss stood up, her face chalk-white, when he came back. Her eyes were fixed on him in what might have been dread. Race halted, forgetting his errand.

"Is something wrong? It's all right; he's dead!"

"Yes. I killed him," she whispered, tonelessly, still staring at him.

Race opened his mouth, closed it. Now he remembered the moan, her anguished expression just before she fired. "You didn't kill him," he said at last. "Not a Starling, not with a gun. I did." Almost, he told her that he couldn't have done it without her distraction.

It was well he didn't. She closed her eyes in relief and the tears started: not drop by drop, but as her eyelids closed a stream of tears poured from each. He had never seen such a thing. She did not even sob. She curled into an anguished ball, face in hands, but he thought there was a note of relief in her moan.

He stared for a moment, slowly becoming aware that it was Slavin's death that wrung her so. He felt as if he had broken something rare and precious and wished Slavin alive again—anything to lighten her anguish. Awkwardly he put an arm around her, groping for words: neither *I'm sorry,* nor *I didn't mean to* were adequate.

He could only stand helplessly, conscious of his heat, the sweat trickling down from his armpits; the animal stink of fear and heat and fury on him. He felt soiled.

Joss took a deep breath and looked up, choking back her tears. "I'm—I'm glad it wasn't me. I prayed I'd shoot the right one, but oh, I didn't know, I didn't know!"

Race stood quivering for long moments while she leaned her head against him and cried more normally.

I didn't know!

Of course not, he thought dazedly. *She had no way of knowing what kind of monster I've become. I did kill a harmless Starling, after all. And all she knew of me was what* he *told her.*

He put both arms around her and held her tight. "Oh Joss, Joss! I thought he was like Macardel! I thought I was *saving* you!"

She had stopped crying, though still the tears flowed. She even smiled, wanly. "No Starling could be that bad." She was silent for a moment, gathering courage. "I'm not going back to him. Even if he is your chief crewman."

"Chief crewman! I killed him, first thing!"

She stared at him, wide-eyed. "But, Geré said—"

All Race's rage at the Starling revived in an instant. She turned pale at his expression. He glared at her. "Did he give you any Starling training?"

Startled, she shook her head. "I'm not a Starling!"

"I am, and you have the same parents. You have as much Starling blood as I." Joquirl had suggested that their ancestors, two hundred years before, had had a drop of Starling blood, which had been concentrated by generations of inbreeding in Ravenham and the surrounding villages.

Incredulous, she said, "But he didn't know you were a Starling! We never told him. He thought that S. Chen had killed you and taken your place—"

Race was shaking his head. "Just a minute ago he called me by name, said I was from the Plantation, and that I had come for my sister. He knew all along. That Chen story shouldn't have fooled you for a moment. He may have been fond of you," he added more gently. "But basically, he hated all humans and he meant to keep you as a slave."

Dazed, she put her hands to her face, staring at nothing.

Race's sense of urgency returned. "I've got to clean up the mess—I need some water and a towel."

She pointed vaguely and murmured directions. Race managed to clean up the worst of the bloodstains. There was another rug in the morning room; he moved it to cover what was left. *No one will miss him till morning, likely; not till some other Starling calls him and doesn't get an answer. At first, they won't believe he's dead. Um—there's a chance he'll be called tonight—he was important and now the whole planet's on watch for me because of his order. We've only got hours to get away.*

Joss wandered in while he was wrapping the towel around the corpse. He tensed, but she showed no reaction, merely stared unseeingly at the swathed head. She'd have to alter all her conceptions of him. Race had no time to help her.

"Let's go, Joss," he said gently. Lifting her with his mind, the corpse on his other side, he retraced the route to the open door. When he shut it, all the lights went out and Joss caught her breath. Race held them there, looking feverishly around the city. Where to hide the body?

At the base of the shaft, of course. Like most of the spires, Slavin Towers was outside the human city; its base was in a landscaped park. Dropping into the dimness, he spotted a heavy stone bench, lifted it quickly, bundled the body under it, and replaced it.

Flinging an arm around Joss, he arrowed for the sky as if afraid that Slavin might awake and hurl himself after them. Joss twisted in his grasp to look back, watching bench and building shaft dwindle behind them half across the bowl valley. They landed on the warehouse roof and Race had to think of why he had come here; he was following his plans unconsciously.

Leaving Joss on the roof, he pried open a door, extracted his shipping containers, and was gone before the guard awoke. Seconds later, they were landing on the roof of the Spanish Casa. He left the containers there and took Joss down to the suite.

She was a stranger. He almost didn't recognize her. So still, so silent, so solemn. Years older. Embarrassed, Race said, "There's food here. Are you thirsty? Have some tea."

With a nervous little start Joss stepped toward the table, murmuring a reply. Race stared at her, conscious of the unnaturalness of his own words. She wasn't hungry or thirsty, but when a Starling suggests, a wise human agrees. She was reacting just as a woman might who'd been picked up by a strange Starling, or not a strange one.

"Hey, Joss—relax," he said, gently but urgently. "I'm your brother—Race. Don't you remember me?"

Her eyes opened and her eyebrows went up in the old, girlish, Jossic way. She turned toward him, startled into a laugh. It was brief and her expression reverted to constraint. "Ye-es. But you *are* a Starling. . . ."

With an obvious effort she approached him, leaned

against his chair solemnly but with a faint sisterly air. After a slight hesitation, she touched his hair.

The warmth of her against his shoulder brought fleetingly but forcefully to Race the sacrifice she had made for him. How had Macardel treated her? The image of his young sister as he had once seen her, nude and serene so long ago, flashed before him. The whole sense of the girl and child she had been swept over him. Lost now, left behind on the other side of that gulf of time and tears that turned her from girl to woman, him from man to Starling. Did that same gulf gape between himself and his mother? He had come home, but home wasn't here.

Mother and sister have I none. . . . He touched her cheek, shaken.

Her arm slid around his shoulders. "Oh, Race, it *is* you, it is you. We never dared hope to see you again. Oh Race, Race. . . ."

Race's eyes burned and he put his arms around her. Perhaps that gulf could be bridged. He was no S. Jackson, nor a Slavin. But even to be an S. Altamont was not enough. He was one of the people, a *man* before he was a Starling. . . . Joss sighed.

Maybe I have come home. . . .

Motion beyond the door alerted him and he flung Joss away—but the three quiet taps could only be Janinda's. She stepped in and smiled at him quite as if she had seen him yesterday—a strong woman, as tall as himself, beauty enhanced by the fine lines around her eyes.

"Hello, Race," she said, and her voice rang with gladness.

"Home the warrior comes," he told her, holding out his arms, his eyes overflowing. She stepped forward and caught him to her as she had not held him since he entered his teens, all their dignity forgotten.

Incredibly, she hadn't changed. Starling or no, he was her son. He heard pride mingling with the gladness in her murmurs—pride of him, not for what she had done for him.

"I couldn't believe it," she murmured, holding him at length to look at him, Joss at her side, looking now like the Joss of old. "When those people mentioned Sturtevant I wouldn't let myself belive it, but I had to find out. I never guessed the old man—such a wonderful man, like Grandfather Sturtevant—was from you."

"Joquirl Wun—my astrogator. The others were the Yales—Hal Yale is crew chief." Glancing at Joss. "Crew chief of the *Nod*." She laughed then—again like her old self.

Glancing at his watch, Race added, "They should be here any time. We've got to hurry. We should be off the planet in three or four hours if things go well."

He was too intent to notice Jocela's eyes light, or that both women looked at him almost worshipfully. He had traveled far and seen many things, and now he spoke thus casually of getting off a planet. . . .

Joss frowned and turned to her mother, sober. "Mother, did you know that Geremé Slavin knew that 'Chen' was really my brother?"

Janinda answered quietly. "Yes, dear; it was obvious that he did."

Whispering in anguish, she asked, "But you never told me?"

After a moment Janinda spoke, still quietly. "I knew we could do nothing for Race. If he survived, he would come for us. If he didn't—it was the best thing I could do for you. Many girls' parents scheme and spend fortunes to give their girls such a chance."

"But not with the Starling chasing their brothers!"

"Even that," said Race somberly. "T've seen a lot of Starlings and how their societies operate. Don't blame your mother, Joss. What else could she do? If I never came back, it was better that you shouldn't know the truth about Slavin. She always does the right thing," he added, "no matter how it hurts."

That pierced their mother's mask. Her eyes filled

with bitter tears. "I've been in constant pain over you both, since you were born," she whispered. "And before that, for your father."

Joss took a deep breath, let it out, and this time Race did see the worshipful look. "Well, it all paid off. And I guess it was worth it. Everything's going to be all right now?" Then she was the very young Joss, who had asked him that question over a skinned knee or a stubbed toe.

"Everything is going to be all right now," he said grimly. "I promise you that—if we can—here they are now."

They entered rather self-consciously, Allison Yale carrying her sleeping son. She looked challengingly at Janinda and with despair at Joss. Joquirl cleared his throat. "Ahem. Yale is sure that Mrs. Worden was followed here, Sir."

Race nodded. "We'll be gone before any trouble can develop—I hope."

"Er—may I ask where, Sir?"

"The Imperial Cluster, first. Far enough to be safe. There, we'll have to outfit. After that—farther out, where we'll have no trouble with the Starlings." For the first time he spoke of his dream. "What I *really* want is a chance to give Starling training to ordinary humans. Because I'm convinced that anyone can do anything I can, if he only knows how."

He looked from one to another, and to his slow-dawning amazement, not a face lit with that hope. Janinda's face was almost expressionless, but faintly disapproving; Joss was frowning, Yale looked worried, Allison shocked—frightened at the upset of the world. Joquirl's mouth was pursed pedantically, his head shaking slowly.

"No, Sir," he said. In his learned phrases, the fear-based respect he showed to Starlings was gone. "Humans are humans and Starlings are Starlings. That was proven on Old Earth, when the first Starlings developed their powers. Only one out of a hundred thousand developed them—thirty thousand Starlings out of a population of three billion—"

"So many!"

"Yes. And with a very high technology, which has never been matched since. But the proportion of Starlings to humans has gone up to one in ten thousand—naturally. As for the Latents," he shook his head, "I doubt if the proportion of Latents in the human population is even one in a million—perhaps not one in ten million. I know of only one other case of a Latent discovering and developing his powers: Kip Tung."

They gasped—all knew the fairy tale.

"Oh, yes, he was real. But Latents are rare, as I said, because they rarely meet and mate, since they were thinned out so long ago. You know that of a Starling's half-breed children, only one out of four will be Starlings. It goes down to one out of sixteen of the children of a pair of half-breeds. The same holds true if they are Latents, not Starlings. So with each Latent-to-human match, the odds go down—and even with half-breeds the odds are but one in four."

Race was white-faced. "Meaning that Joss isn't a—Latent."

Apologetically he said, "Almost certainly not, Sir."

"Of course not! Do you think I didn't try?" Joss said.

Still he wouldn't give up. "Maybe they didn't go at it the right way. I knew how."

Again Joquirl shook his head. "No, Sir. In those days they had a great science of the mind. With their machines, they learned that there are three main kinds of minds. There is the abstract mind, like mine and those of many mathematicians and philosophers; this kind of mind deals best with words and ideas. Then there is the visual mind, such as yours and many artists'; this kind has great visual memory and grasp of shapes and physical forms—color too. And the most common kind of mind is a mixture of the two, with an average grasp both of ideas and images."

"You're saying that a Starling has to have a ... visual mind?"

"Yes, Sir. And not only that, but more than common powers of concentration. All Starlings are of this mental type, and are of fairly high intelligence—though genius is as rare among them as among humans. Which means that most geniuses are human. But there are *no* Starling half-wits or morons—or even men of low-ordinary minds. Of course," he added, "they breed such. But these lack Starling powers, though some of the low-ordinaries have the Starling sense."

Unwilling though Race was to accept it, he could not help remembering how he thought—mostly in pictures. He had outwitted Slavin not by thinking about what he would likely do, but by picturing him doing it. He had always known that both Joss and Janinda could think circles around him; his method might be as good as theirs—if he was smart enough to be a Starling, as Joquirl implied—but it was slower.

He nodded slowly, bitterly, but protested, "There has to be some way that Starlings and humans can live together! We're all men!"

That embarrassed them. They glanced at each other and Joquirl again pursed his lips, shook his head.

Janinda's eyes were warm. "It's very like you to think it, but we can't turn the galaxy upside down. Don't worry about it. We know *you* will always treat us well. Hadn't we better be moving now? Can you really carry us all?"

"The Imperial Cluster!" Joss whispered, eyes shining.

Race looked at them, one after another. All looked back, eagerly, admiringly, reverently. With a sudden movement he turned and walked to the window, as sick with disappointment as a small boy. He stood looking out into the night, his back to them: they made not a sound. For a moment, he felt like throwing himself out.

Then he realized to him it was not a window, but a

door . . . he was a Starling. But he was also a man! He was *still* a man.

But how long can I remain human if they all insist on worshipping me?

Outstanding science fiction and fantasy

To order these titles,

use coupon on the

last page of this book.

Attention:

DAW COLLECTORS

Many readers of DAW Books have written requesting information on early titles and book numbers to assist in the collection of DAW editions since the first of our titles appeared in April 1972.

We have prepared a several-pages-long list of all DAW titles, giving their sequence numbers, original and current order numbers, and ISBN numbers. And of course the authors and book titles, as well as reissues.

If you think that this list will be of help, you may have a copy by writing to the address below and enclosing fifty cents in stamps or coins to cover the handling and postage costs.

DAW BOOKS, INC. Dept. C
1633 Broadway
New York, N.Y. 10019

Presenting JACK VANCE in DAW editions:

The "Demon Princes" Novels

- [ ] STAR KING   #UE1402—$1.75
- [ ] THE KILLING MACHINE   #UE1409—$1.75
- [ ] THE PALACE OF LOVE   #UE1442—$1.75
- [ ] THE FACE   #UJ1498—$1.95
- [ ] THE BOOK OF DREAMS   #UE1587—$2.25

The "Tschai" Novels

- [ ] CITY OF THE CHASCH   #UE1461—$1.75
- [ ] SERVANTS OF THE WANKH   #UE1467—$1.75
- [ ] THE DIRDIR   #UE1478—$1.75
- [ ] THE PNUME   #UE1484—$1.75

The "Alastor" Trilogy

- [ ] TRULLION: ALASTOR 2262   #UE1590—$2.25
- [ ] MARUNE: ALASTOR 933   #UE1591—$2.25
- [ ] WYST: ALASTOR 1716   #UE1593—$2.25

Others

- [ ] EMPHYRIO   #UE1504—$2.25
- [ ] THE FIVE GOLD BANDS   #UJ1518—$1.95
- [ ] THE MANY WORLDS OF MAGNUS RIDOLPH   #UE1531—$1.75
- [ ] THE LANGUAGES OF PAO   #UE1541—$1.75
- [ ] NOPALGARTH   #UE1563—$2.25
- [ ] DUST OF FAR SUNS   #UE1588—$1.75

If You wish to order these titles,

please see the coupon in

the back of this book.

Presenting C. J. CHERRYH

☐ **DOWNBELOW STATION.** A blockbuster of a novel! Interstellar warfare as humanity's colonies rise in cosmic rebellion. (#UE1594—$2.75)

☐ **SERPENT'S REACH.** Two races lived in harmony in a quarantined constellation—until one person broke the truce! (#UE1554—$2.25)

☐ **FIRES OF AZEROTH.** Armageddon at the last gate of three worlds. (#UJ1466—$1.95)

☐ **HUNTER OF WORLDS.** Triple fetters of the mind served to keep their human prey in bondage to this city-sized starship. (#UE1559—$2.25)

☐ **BROTHERS OF EARTH:** This in-depth novel of an alien world and a human who had to adjust or die was a Science Fiction Book Club Selection. (#UJ1470—$1.95)

☐ **THE FADED SUN: KESRITH.** Universal praise for this novel of the last members of humanity's warrior-enemies . . . and the Earthman who was fated to save them. (#UE1600—$2.25)

☐ **THE FADED SUN: SHON'JIR.** Across the untracked stars to the forgotten world of the Mri go the last of that warrior race and the man who had betrayed humanity. (#UE1632—$2.25)

☐ **THE FADED SUN: KUTATH.** The final and dramatic conclusion of this bestselling trilogy—with three worlds in militant confrontation. (#UE1516—$2.25)

☐ **HESTIA.** A single engineer faces the terrors and problems of an endangered colony planet. (#UJ1488—$1.95)

DAW BOOKS are represented by the publisher of Signet and Mentor Books, THE NEW AMERICAN LIBRARY, INC.